The Conscript

SALZWASSER
VERLAG

M. Erckmann-Chatrian

The Conscript

Reprint of the original, first published in 1865.

1st Edition 2022 | ISBN: 978-3-75258-996-2

Verlag (Publisher): Salzwasser Verlag GmbH, Zeilweg 44, 60439 Frankfurt, Deutschland
Vertretungsberechtigt (Authorized to represent): E. Roepke, Zeilweg 44, 60439 Frankfurt, Deutschland
Druck (Print): Books on Demand GmbH, In de Tarpen 42, 22848 Norderstedt, Deutschland

THE CONSCRIPT:

A

TALE OF THE FRENCH WAR OF 1813.

TRANSLATED FROM THE FRENCH OF M. ERCKMANN CHATRIAN.

WITH A FRONTISPIECE.

LONDON

1865.

TRANSLATOR'S PREFACE.

The interest of this narrative, and its wide popularity in France, where it has been received almost as a veritable piece of Autobiography, induced the Translator to think that this story of a Conscript would be acceptable to English readers. It is never a useless task to set before our eyes the horrors of war; and the present times, rife with wars or rumours of wars, make us feel that the lesson taught by the following pages, is needed still.

A Translation of the Conscript's account of the Campaign of Waterloo, forming a sequel to the present volume, will shortly appear. The popularity of the latter work, now in its Tenth Edition, has already nearly equalled that of its predecessor, of which sixteen thousand copies have been sold.

THE CONSCRIPT:

A TALE OF THE FRENCH WAR.

CHAPTER I.

Those who have not seen the glory of the Emperor Napoleon in the years 1810, 1811, 1812, will never know to what height of power a man can rise.

When he passed through Champagne, Lorraine or Alsace, people in the midst of the harvest or the vintage would abandon everything to run and meet him; they would come from eight or ten leagues off; women, children, old men, threw themselves in his way, crying with uplifted hands—"Vive l'Empereur! vive l'Empereur!" One would have thought he was a God, that he kept the world going, that if by mischance he died all would be over with us. Some ancient

Republicans, who shook their heads, and permitted themselves to say, over their bottle, that the Emperor *might* fall, passed for madmen. This appeared against nature, and could not be thought of for a moment.

As for me, I had been apprenticed, since 1804, to the old clockmaker, Melchior Goulden, at Phalsbourg. As I appeared weakly and limped a little, my mother wished me to learn some quieter business than those of our village; for at Dagsberg are to be found only wood-cutters, charcoal-burners, and sledge-makers. M. Goulden was very fond of me. We lived on the first floor of the great corner house fronting the *Bœuf Rouge,* and near the French gate.

It was a sight to see the princes, ambassadors, and generals stop there—some on horseback, some in calèches, some in chariots, with braided coats, plumes, furs, and all kinds of national decorations. And on the high-road it was worth while seeing the trains of couriers, messengers, convoys of ammunition, guns, waggons, cavalry, and infantry! What stirring times!

In five or six years George the landlord had made his fortune; he owned fields, orchards, houses, and money in abundance: for all these people coming from Germany, Switzerland, Russia, Poland, or elsewhere, made nothing of a few handfuls of gold which they scattered on the high-roads: they were all nobles who took a sort of pride in never counting the cost.

From morning till evening, and even during the night, the hotel of the Bœuf Rouge kept open house. All along the high windows of the ground-floor you saw tables spread with great white table-cloths, sparkling with plate and covered with game, fish, and other delicacies, round which these travellers took their places. You heard nothing in the great court-yard at the back but the neighing of horses, the shouts of postilions, the loud laughter of servants, and the roll of carriages coming and going through the lofty entrance-gates. Ah, the hotel of the Bœuf Rouge will never have such a flourishing time again!

There, too, would come townspeople whom we had known formerly as picking up sticks in the forests, or working as scavengers on the high-roads: they had come to be commandants, colonels, and generals, one in a thousand of them, all through having fought in almost every country of the world.

Old Melchior, with his black silk cap pulled down over his great hairy ears, with his heavy eyelids, his nose squeezed in his great horn spectacles, and his lips compressed, could not help sometimes laying down his glass and his awl on the counter to give a glance at the inn; especially when the postilions, with their ponderous boots, short jackets, and hempen wigs frizzled on the back of their heads, made the echoes of the ramparts resound with the loud crack of their whips, to announce some arrival. Then he would become attentive, and from time to time I could hear him cry out,—

"Look, there's the son of Jacob the tiler; of Marie-Anne, the old butcher; or of Franz Lepel, the cooper. He has got on; now he is a colonel and baron of the empire into the bargain! Why don't he take up his quarters with his father there, down in the Rue des Capucines?"

But whenever he saw them take the direction of the street, shaking hands to right and left with their old acquaintances, his countenance would change, as he wiped his eyes with his coarse checked handkerchief, and murmured,—

"Poor old Annette! she is going to have a great pleasure! That's right—that's right! He at least is not proud—he's a fine fellow—if he only doesn't get knocked on the head with a cannon-ball one of these days!"

Some passed as if ashamed to recognize their homes, others traversed the town proudly to go and see a sister or cousin. Everybody talked about *them:* one would have said all Phalsbourg wore their decoration and their epaulettes; as for the first, they were as much or more despised than when they swept the high-roads.

Almost every month Te Deums were sung for some great victory, and the cannon of the arsenal fired one-and-twenty-gun salutes, which made one's heart throb. For six weeks after, every family was in anxiety; the poor old women, especially, looked out for letters: the first that came was heard of by all the town. "Such a one has received news of her Jacques, or her Claude!"—and all ran to know if anything was said of their Joseph, or their Jean Baptiste. I don't speak of promotions or notices of deaths; promotions every one believed in, for the dead must be replaced; but for the lists of casualties the parents waited weeping, for they did not come directly: sometimes they did not come at all, and the poor old people kept on hoping, thinking, "Perhaps our lad is a prisoner; when peace is made, he will return. How many have come back who were thought dead!" But peace was never made; as soon as one war was finished another was begun. There was always something we wanted, either from Russia, or Spain, or elsewhere: the Emperor was never contented.

Often, at sight of the regiments who marched through the town—the foot soldiers with their long coats tucked up round the hips, knapsacks on their backs, their long gaiters reaching up to the knee, and their weapons sloped, walking with long strides, sometimes covered with mud, sometimes white with dust—often would Father Melchior musingly say to me—

"Tell me, Joseph, how many of them do you think we have seen pass since 1804?"

"Oh, I don't know, M. Goulden," I said; "at least four or five hundred thousand."

"Ay, at least!" he answered. "And how many have you seen return?"

I understood him then, but I answered—

"Perhaps they return by Mayence, or some other route. Surely it cannot be otherwise?"

But he shook his head, and said—

"Those whom you have not seen come back are dead, as hundreds of thousands of others will die, if God does not take pity on us; for the Emperor loves nothing but war! He has already shed more blood to give crowns to his brothers than our great Revolution did to obtain the Rights of Man."

M. Goulden's reflections set me, too, reflecting with no little anxiety. I was slightly lame of the left leg, it was true; but how many others with infirmities had got their marching orders all the same?

These ideas ran in my head so as to give me great distress. I was terrified, not only because I did not like war, but still more because I wished to marry my cousin Catherine of Quatre Vents. We had been in a manner brought up together. She was the most blooming, smiling girl you would wish to see: blonde, with pretty blue eyes, rosy cheeks, and teeth white as milk: she was nearly eighteen years old, I was nineteen; and my aunt Margrédel seemed pleased to see me come early every Sunday to breakfast and dine with them.

Catherine and I used to go to the orchard at the back of the house; we ate together the apples and pears, and were the happiest creatures in the world. It was my duty, too, to take her to mass and vespers, and at fêtes she never quitted my arm, refusing to dance with the other village lads. All the world knew that we were to be married one day; but if I had to go as a conscript all would be over. A thousand times I wished I were much lamer; for at that time they would take first the single men, next the married men without family, and then the married men with one child. In spite of myself I thought, " Surely, the lame are better worth taking than fathers of families? can they not put them in the cavalry?" This idea made me so sad that I would fain have run away.

But it was principally in 1812, at the beginning of the war with Russia, that my fear increased. From the month of February to the end of May, every day we saw nothing but regiments on regiments pass by—dragoons, cuirassiers, carabineers, hussars, lancers, artillery, powder-chests, ambulances, carriages, provisions—for ever and ever, like a stream flowing on without ceasing.

I remember even now, that these were preceded by grenadiers who drove great waggons drawn by oxen. These oxen were employed instead of horses, that they might serve for food afterwards, when the supplies were used up. " What a good idea!" people said. " When the grenadiers can no longer feed the oxen, the oxen will feed the grenadiers." Unluckily those who spoke thus did not know that oxen can only go seven or eight leagues a day, and that they require at least one day of rest to eight of marching; so that these poor beasts with their horns already worn out, their lips drivelling, their eyes starting out of their heads, their necks sunk in their shoulders, had nothing remaining of them but skin and bone. For three weeks did these poor creatures pass, all mangled with bayonet wounds. Meat became cheap, for many of these oxen were slaughtered; but few would buy, diseased meat being unwholesome: yet they only came from twenty leagues on the other side the Rhine.

Afterwards we saw defile by, only lances, sabres and helmets, all of which were swallowed up by the French gate, then they traversed the Place d'Armes, and issued out by the German gate.

At last, on the 10th of May in the year 1812, very early in the morning, the guns of the arsenal announced the master of all. I was still sleeping when the first volley was discharged, making my small window-panes rattle like a drum; almost immediately after M. Goulden, with a lighted candle, opened my door, saying—

"Get up—there he is!"

We opened the window. Through the dark I saw advancing at a hard trot under the French gate above a hundred dragoons, many of whom carried torches; they passed with a terrible rolling and stampings; the lights played on the fronts of the houses, and from all the windows were heard ceaseless cries of "Vive l'Empereur!"

A horse came down suddenly at the stake of the butcher Klein, used for fastening up the oxen, and the dragoon fell in a heap with his head in the gutter; immediately a head leant forward out of the carriage to see what was the matter—a large, fat, pale face, with a tuft of hair on the forehead. It was Napoleon. He held up his hand as if to take a pinch of snuff, and spoke some words in an abrupt tone. The officer who gallopped beside the carriage-window bent down to answer him. He took his pinch and the carriage turned the corner. That was all I saw.

The Emperor did not stop at Phalsbourg. Whilst he proceeded on the road to Savenne, the cannon discharged their last volleys. Then silence returned—the guard at the French gate drew up the bridge, and the old clock-maker said to me, "You saw?"

"Yes, Monsieur Goulden!"

"Well," he said, "that man holds all our lives in his hand; let us thank Heaven that he is not bad-hearted, or the world would see frightful things, as in the times of the barbarous kings and the Turks." Then he added, "You can go to bed again; there's three o'clock striking."

From that day to the end of September, many a Te Deum was sung in the church, and twenty-one-gun salutes were fired for every new victory: then M. Goulden would exclaim—

"Ha, Joseph! another battle won! 50,000 men killed, 25 standards and 100 pieces taken! All goes well—very well! It only remains to raise a new levy to replace those who are dead!"

In the morning he opened my door: I saw him all bald and grey, in his shirt-sleeves, with his neck bare, washing his face in the basin.

"Do you really think, M. Goulden," I said to him in great distress, "that they will take the lame?"

"No, no," said he kindly: "don't be afraid, my boy; you really could not serve: we will arrange all that for you. Do you work hard, and don't trouble yourself about anything else."

He saw my uneasiness, and was sorry for me. I have never met with a better man. Then he dressed himself to go and regulate the clocks of the town, of the Commandant and the Maire, as well as other notable persons. As for me, I stayed within. M. Goulden did not return home till after the Te Deum; he took off his great brown coat, put his wig away in its box, and pulled his silk cap over his ears once more, saying—

"The army is at Wilna—or perhaps at Smolensk; I have just learnt as much at the Commandant's. God grant we may get the better of them this once more, and that peace may be made: the sooner the better, for war is a terrible thing."

I thought also, that if we had peace there would be no more such need of men, and I could marry Catherine. Every one may imagine for himself how many prayers I put up for the glory of the Emperor.

CHAPTER II.

It was on the 15th of September that we learnt our great victory of the Moskowa. All the world was in a state of jubilation, and cried out, "Now we are going to have peace—now the war is finished!"

Some good-for-nothing fellows said that it only remained to get hold of China: one finds people of that kind to make one miserable.

Eight days afterwards, it was known that we had reached Moscow, the largest and richest city in Russia, and it was thought that this would diminish the conscriptions. But soon the rumour ran that the Russians had set their city on fire, and that we should be obliged to retreat upon Poland, if we did not wish to perish of famine. Nothing was spoken of but this in the inns, the breweries, the corn markets, everywhere: people could not meet without saying straightway, "Well—well! 'tis a bad job—the retreat is begun!"

People turned pale, and hundreds of peasants waited

at the post-office from morning till night; but no letters came. I, for my part, passed through all this crowd without taking much notice: I had seen so much of it! Besides, I had an idea which rejoiced my heart and made me see everything in rose-colour.

You must know that for five months I had been wanting to make Catherine a splendid present for her birthday, which was on the 18th of December. Amongst the watches in M. Goulden's shop window, there was a very small one, exceedingly pretty, with a silver cap, and streaked with little circles which made it shine like a star. Round the face, under the glass, was a network of copper, and on the face were painted two lovers making some kind of declaration: the young man was giving the girl a great nosegay of roses, for which she held out her hand, casting her eyes modestly down.

The first time I had seen this watch, I said to myself, "I must not let it escape me; it shall be Catherine's. If I'm forced to work every day till midnight, I *must* have it." M. Goulden, after seven o'clock, let me work on my own account. We had old watches to clean, set right, or mount afresh; this was a troublesome business, and when I had done that kind of work, Father Melchior paid me accordingly.

But the little watch cost thirty-five francs. It may be imagined then, what hours of the night I should have to pass to get it. I am sure that if M. Goulden had known that I wanted it, he would have made me a present of it; but I should not have allowed a penny to be taken off; I should have looked on that as disgraceful: I said to myself, "I *must* earn it—nobody shall be able to say a word on that score." Only, lest another should have the idea of buying it, I put it aside in a box, telling Father Melchior that I knew a purchaser for that watch.

It will now be easily understood that all these stories about the war went in at one ear and out at the other. While working I pictured to myself Catherine's delight: for five months I had nothing else before my eyes. I fancied her look when she should receive my present, and I asked myself, "What will she say?" Sometimes I fancied she would exclaim, "Oh, Joseph, what can you be thinking of? 'Tis too fine for me. No, no, I can't accept such a beautiful watch!" Then I force her to take it; I slip it into her apron-pocket, saying, "Come, come, Catherine—do you wish to vex me?"—I see that she wishes for it and that she says this by way of seeming to refuse it. Sometimes I pictured her blushing all over; she raises her hands, saying, "Good God! now, Joseph, I *know* that you love me!" and she kisses me, with tears in her eyes. I am so happy, and Aunt Grédel approves of it all. In short, a thousand such ideas passed through my mind, and at night, when I went to bed, I thought, "Well, there isn't a man so happy as you are, Joseph! Now you can make Catherine a rare present of your own earning. And surely she will prepare something for *your* birth-day, for she thinks only of you; you are both happy, and when you are married all will go well." These thoughts softened me: never had I experienced such satisfaction.

While I was thus working, thinking only of my happiness, the winter arrived sooner than usual: towards the beginning of November. It did not begin with the snow, but with great cold and hard frosts. In a few days all the leaves had fallen, the earth hardened like stone, and everything was covered with hoar-frost: roofs, pavements, window-panes. We had to have fires that year to keep the cold from entering through the chinks! If the door was left open a moment, all the heat escaped; the wood sparkled in the stove; it burned and crackled like straw, and the chimneys drew well.

Every morning I hastened to wipe the windows of the shop-front with hot water, and scarcely had I shut the windows again than a coating of frost covered them. One heard people outside running and breathing hard, with their faces in their coat-collars, and their hands in their pockets. No one stopped, and the house-doors were quickly shut again.

I don't know what became of the sparrows, whether they were dead or living, but not a single one chirped on the house-tops, and but for the 'réveil' and 'retraite' played at the two barracks, no noise broke the silence.

Often when the fire blazed well, M. Goulden would stop all at once in his work, and looking for an instant at the white panes, would exclaim,—

"Our poor soldiers! our poor soldiers!"

He said this in so sad a voice that I felt a pang at my heart, and replied,—

"But M. Goulden, they must now be in Poland in good barracks; for to think that human beings can support such cold is impossible."

"Such cold!" he said; "yes, in this country it is cold, very cold, on account of the currents of mountain air; and yet what is this cold to that of the North in Poland and Russia? God grant they have started early enough! Good heaven! what a heavy charge have they who govern men!"

Then he was silent, and for hours I thought of what he had said to me; I pictured to myself our soldiers on their way, running to warm themselves. But the idea of Catherine always came back to me, and I have often thought afterwards that when people are happy, the unhappiness of others touches them but little; especially in youth, when the passions are strongest, and the experience of great misfortunes is still wanting to you.

After the frost, so much snow fell that the couriers were stopped in the direction of Quatre Vents. I was afraid that I might not be able to go to Catherine on her birthday, but two companies of infantry went out with pickaxes and cut in the hard snow a road for the carriages, and this road lasted till the beginning of the month of April, 1813.

However Catherine's fête was coming nearer every day, and my happiness increased in proportion. I had got the thirty-five francs, but I did not know how to say to M. Goulden that I would buy the watch. I should have liked to keep these things secret; it was so disagreeable to me to talk about them.

At last the evening before the fête, between six or seven o'clock, as we sat working in silence, the lamp between us, I took my resolution on a sudden and said—

"You know, M. Goulden, that I have spoken to you about a purchaser for the little silver-watch?"

"Yes, Joseph," he answered tranquilly; "but he hasn't come yet."

"I am the purchaser, M. Goulden."

He raised his head quite astonished. I drew out the thirty-five francs and laid them on the counter. He looked at me.

"But," said he, "that's not a watch for you, Joseph; what you want is a good big watch which will fill your pocket well and mark the seconds. Those little watches are for women."

I did not know what to say.

M. Goulden, after musing a few instants, began to smile.

"Ah, ha! very good!" he said; "now I understand: it's Catherine's fête! So that's why you have been working night and day. Come, take back this money: I don't want any of it."

I was quite confused.

"I thank you very much, M. Goulden," I said;

"but this watch is for Catherine, and I am very glad to have earned the purchase-money. You would give me pain by refusing the money: I would just as soon let the watch go."

He said no more, and took the thirty-five francs; then he opened a drawer, and chose a fine steel chain with two little silver gilt keys which he fixed to the watch, enclosing the whole in a little box with a pink favour. He did it slowly, and as if with some emotion, and then he gave me the box.

"It's a pretty present, Joseph," he said; "Catherine ought to reckon herself lucky in having a lover like you. She is a good girl. Now we can go to supper: get the table ready while I take the pot off the fire."

This was done; then M. Goulden took from the cupboard a bottle of his Metz wine, which he kept for great occasions, and we supped, in a manner, like two comrades: for through the whole evening he ceased not to talk of the happy days of his youth, saying that he had formerly had a sweetheart, but that in the year '92 he had gone with the general levy on account of the Prussian invasion, and that on his return to Fenétrange he had found this person married: which was natural enough, as he had never permitted himself to tell her his love;

but this had not prevented him from remaining faithful to that tender remembrance: he spoke of it very seriously. I meanwhile listened, thinking of Catherine, and it was not till at the stroke of ten, when the watch went their rounds—the great cold causing them to be relieved every twenty minutes—that we put two large logs in the stove and went to bed.

CHAPTER III.

THE next day, the 18th December, I awoke about six o'clock in the morning. It was terribly cold; my windows were perfectly coated with frost.

I had taken care the night before to hang out on the back of a chair my sky-blue swallow-tailed coat, my trowsers, my chamois-leather waistcoat, a white shirt, and my fine black silk cravat. All was ready; my stockings and well-blacked shoes were at the foot of the bed, and I had but to put on my clothes. Nevertheless the cold I felt in my face, the sight of the window-panes, and the deep silence outside, made me shiver beforehand. Had it not been Catherine's fête, I should have remained there till midday; but all of a sudden that idea made me jump out of bed and run very quickly to the great china-stove, where there were almost always remaining some embers of the evening before in the cinders. I found two or three, which I hastily collected together, and putting at the top some sticks and two large logs, I plunged again into bed.

M. Goulden, under his great curtains, the counterpane drawn up to his nose, and his cotton nightcap over his eyes, had just waked; he heard me, and cried,—

"Joseph, there has not been such cold weather for forty years. I feel it. What a winter we are going to have!"

I answered nothing; I lay looking to see if the fire burned. It took more than half-an-hour to warm the air; at last I rose and dressed. At eight o'clock I was about to go out, when M. Goulden exclaimed,—

"Joseph, what are you thinking of? Are you going in that dress-coat to Quatre Vents. Why, you'll be dead halfway. Come into my room, take a large cloak, mufflers, and flannel-soled shoes."

I hesitated, I thought myself so finely dressed; but he went on,—

"Listen—a man was yesterday found frozen to death on the way to Wechem. Dr. Steinbrenner said he sounded like a piece of dry wood when they rapped him. It was a soldier: he had left the village between six and seven o'clock; at eight o'clock they picked him up—

short work you see. If you wish to have your nose and ears frozen, you have only to go out like that."

I saw that he was right; so I put on his great shoes, mufflers and cloak, and went out; he warning me not to be late back, because of the cold, and because a great number of wolves would have crossed the Rhine on the ice.

The cold was so keen, that the air seemed full of needles, and one shivered spite of oneself from head to foot. Under the German gate, I saw the sentry in his great grey cloak, withdrawn like a saint to the inside of his niche; he held his musket with his sleeve that his fingers might not be frozen against the steel; two icicles hung from his moustache. No one was at the bridge nor at the toll-gate. A little further, I saw two carriages in the middle of the road, fastened down as close as hampers and sparkling with frost; they had had the horses taken out and been abandoned. Everything seemed dead; one heard only the ice crackle under one's feet.

I folded the cloak against my chest, hid my nose in the fur collar, plunged my hands in the mufflers up to my elbows, and ran as hard as I could along the great trench the soldiers had cut from the town to Quatre

Vents. The walls were of ice; in some parts swept by the north wind: one could see the ravine of Fiquet, the oak-forest, and the blue mountains—all brought near by the clearness of the air. The farm-dogs barked no more, it was too cold for them.

In spite of all, the thought of Catherine warmed my heart, and soon I discovered the first houses of Quatre Vents. The chimneys and the thatched roofs on either side scarcely rose above the mounds of snow, and the people had cut a trench along the walls to the end of the village to get to each other. But to-day every family kept round its own hearth, and the little round panes of glass seemed pricked with a red point, from the light of the large fires inside. Before every door was a pile of straw to keep the cold from coming in.

At the fourth door I stopped, took off my mufflers, opened it, and shut it quickly again. This was the house of my aunt Grédel Bauer, the widow of Mathias Bauer and the mother of Catherine.

As I entered shivering, Aunt Grédel, seated before the fire, turned in surprise at my great fur collar. Catherine in her Sunday dress, with a fine striped skirt, a fringed handkerchief crossed over her bosom, the strings of her red apron tied round her slim waist, and a pretty blue silk cap bound with black velvet encircling her fair and blooming face, her soft eyes and slightly turned-up nose—Catherine cried out, "'Tis Joseph!"

And without looking twice, she ran to embrace me, saying—

"I *knew* the cold would not prevent you from coming."

I was so happy that I could not speak! I took off my mantle and hung it up; I took off the great shoes, and felt myself quite pale with happiness.

I tried to find something agreeable to say, but as it did not come, I said all of a sudden—

"See, Catherine, here's something for your fête; but first you must kiss me once more before opening the box."

She turned to me her pretty rosy cheeks, and then approaching the table, unfastened the string, and opened the box. I was behind, and my heart went pit-a-pat: I feared lest the watch should not be handsome enough. But in an instant Catherine joined her hands and sighed out quite low—

"Oh, how beautiful! It's a watch."

"Yes," said Aunt Grédel, "it is most beautiful: one would say it was of silver."

"But it *is* of silver," said Catherine, looking at me inquiringly.

Then I said, "Do you really, Aunt Grédel, think me capable of giving a watch of plated copper to the girl I love more than my own life? If I were capable of it, I should despise myself as the dirt under my feet."

Catherine hearing this, put her two arms round my neck, and as we thus stood I said to myself, "This is the happiest day of my life!"

Aunt Grédel was soon busy at the hearth, coming and going to prepare pancakes, with dried prunes, and little cakes dipped in wine spiced with cinnamon, and other good things; and at last when she cried joyously, "Come, children, to table!" we saw the clean white cloth, the great soup-tureen, the pitcher of wine, and the great pancake, round and golden, on a large dish in the middle. We sat and ate with a good appetite. Outside nothing was to be heard; the fire crackled on the hearth: it was very comfortable in this spacious kitchen. The grey cat, rather wild, looked at us from a distance across the balustrade of the staircase without venturing down.

After dinner Catherine sang the air, "Du lieber Gott!" She had a sweet voice, which went up to heaven. I sang in a low voice just to accompany her. Aunt Grédel was spinning, and the click of the wheel filled up the pauses: we were all touched. When one air was done we began another. At three o'clock my aunt served us the spiced cakes; we ate together, laughing like fools, and my aunt pretending to scold us. This went on till four o'clock, when it began to grow dark, and thinking that we must soon part, we sat sadly beside the hearth, where the red flame was dancing. Catherine pressed my hand; I, sitting with bended head, would have given my life to stay. At last Aunt Grédel cried, "Joseph, it's time you were gone. The moon does not rise till midnight, and it will soon be as black as an oven. You will come again on Sunday."

I put on again the mantle, mufflers, and overshoes. I embraced them both. Catherine reminded me to come again on Sunday, and I set off running without raising my head, for the cold filled my eyes with tears.

I had been going on thus twenty minutes, scarcely daring to breathe, when a hoarse, tipsy voice called to me from a distance, "Who goes there?"

I looked into the grey darkness, and I saw, fifty

paces before me, the hawker, Pinacle, with his great basket, his otter-skin cap, his woollen gloves, and his iron-pointed stick. The lantern, hanging to the basket-strap, lighted up his drunken face, his bristly yellow-bearded chin, and his great nose shaped like an extinguisher. He glared with his little eyes like a wolf, repeating, "Who goes there?"

This Pinacle was the greatest rascal in the country. He had even the year before got into a scrape with M. Goulden, who demanded from him the price of a watch that he had undertaken to deliver to M. Anstett, the curate of Homert; for, having received the money, he had put it in his pocket, saying he had paid it to me. But though this jackanapes swore it before the magistrate, M. Goulden very well knew the contrary, for since that day neither he nor I had left the house. Besides this, Pinacle having wanted to dance with Catherine at the fête at Quatre Bras, she had refused; because she knew the story of the watch, and because, besides, she always remained on my arm.

The rascal, who was very spiteful, owed me therefore a grudge; and to see him there, all of a sudden, in the middle of the road, far from the town and all help, with his service-wood stick and its iron point, did not much rejoice me. However, the little path which winds round the burial-ground lay to my left, and, without answering, I hastened to run along it, with the snow almost up to my waist.

Whereupon he, guessing who I was, cried furiously, "Ah, ah! 'tis the little cripple! Halt, halt! I must wish you good evening. You come from Catherine, you watch-stealer!"

I sprang like a hare over the heaps of snow. He tried at first to follow me, but his basket impeded him; whereupon, seeing that I gained on him, he put his two hands to his mouth, shouting—

"It don't matter, cripple, you'll be settled nevertheless: the conscription is coming—the great conscription of the blind, and the lame, and the humpbacked. You'll go, and you'll be left behind out yonder like the others."

Then he went on his way, laughing like a drunkard as he was; while I, having scarcely strength to breathe, regained the road at the entrance to the *glacis*, thanking heaven that I had found the little path so near; for this Pinacle, who was notorious for drawing out his knife every time he was attacked, might easily have dealt me a dangerous wound.

In spite of my hurried pace, I felt my feet numbed within their thick shoes, and I began again to run. That night the water froze in the cisterns of Phalsbourg, and the wine in the cellars; a thing that had not happened for sixty years.

At the first bridge, and under the German gate, the silence seemed to me still greater than it was in the morning. All along the street I met not a single soul, and when I reached our little alley, it seemed to me quite warm there, though the little gutter in the court was frozen. When I opened my chamber door the pleasant warmth from the stove rejoiced me. M. Goulden sat by the fire in the easy chair, his hands on his knees. Whilst I took off and put away my things, he said—

"Have you been well amused, Joseph?"

"Oh, yes! Aunt Grédel and Catherine send you their compliments."

"Well, well! so much the better!" said he; "the young are right to amuse themselves, for when one becomes old, by dint of having suffered—having seen acts of injustice and selfishness, and misfortunes—everything is spoiled beforehand."

He said this to himself, looking at the fire. I had never seen him so sad, and I asked him—

"Are you ill, M. Goulden?"

Without answering me, he murmured—

"Ay, that's what they are—the great military nations—that's glory!"

He shook his head and sat quite bowed down in thought, his grey eyebrows knitted. Then raising his head he said—

"At this moment, Joseph, there are 400,000 families weeping in France: our great army has perished in the frozen plains of Russia. All those young and vigorous men whom we have for two months been seeing pass, are buried in the snow. The news came this afternoon. Terrible to think of!"

I was silent; what I saw most clearly was that we should soon have a new conscription, as after all the campaigns, and that this time the lame might come in for it. The thought turned me pale.

I went into my room and to bed. For a long while I could not close my eyes, thinking of the conscription, of Catherine, and of all these thousands of men buried in the snow, and saying to myself, that I should do well to escape to Switzerland.

CHAPTER IV.

When next morning, about seven o'clock, I entered M. Goulden's chamber, to set myself to work, he was still in bed and very dejected.

"Joseph," he said to me, "I am not well; all these dreadful stories have made me ill: I have not slept."

"Shall I make you some tea?" I asked.

"No, my boy, no; only make up the fire a little. I shall get up presently. But this is the hour for setting all the clocks in the town: it's Monday, you know. But I can't go; for to see so many good people in such misery would do for me quite. So, Joseph, take the keys hanging there behind the door, and go: that will be best; and if I could sleep an hour or two, it would do me good."

So I put wood on the fire, took mantle and mufflers, and went out with the keys. I was certainly sorry for Father Melchior's being ill, but was consoled by this idea—"I shall get up to the top of the bell-tower, and see from there Catherine's house."

Thus thinking, I arrived at Brainstein's, the bell-ringer, who lived in an old tumble-down shed at the corner of the small Place: his two sons were weavers, and from morning till night might be heard in this hole the creaking of looms and whistling of shuttles. The grandmother, so old that her eyes were no longer to be seen, slept in an old armchair, on the top of which perched a magpie. Old Brainstein, when he had no bells to ring for a christening, a burial, or a marriage, read his almanack behind the little round window-panes.

I arrived then at Brainstein's, and old Brainstein, rising and saluting me, put on his old jacket and woollen cap, driving away the cat who was sleeping on them; he took his great key and we went out. I was happy, in spite of the cold, to be in the open air, for all was murky with steam in this hole, and one could breathe no better than in a seething pot. I could never understand how people could live in such a manner.

At last we went up the street, and old Brainstein said to me,—

"You know the great disaster in Russia, Master Joseph. Ah! it's terrible: but it will bring many masses to the church, for you see all the world will have to get masses said for their children; so much the more because they died in a land of heathens."

As we passed through the place, we saw several persons, peasants and townspeople, standing opposite the guard-house, reading a placard. We entered the church, where, despite the frightful cold, more than twenty persons, young and old, were kneeling on the pavement. Brainstein said that he was sure the half of them had been there since five o'clock.

He opened the little door in the tower, by which you ascend to the organ-loft, and we began to climb in the dark, and got up at last to the bells.

I was very glad to see again the blue sky, and breathe the fresh air, for the bad smell of the bats, in these dark narrow passages, almost stifled one. But how dreadfully cold it was in this cage, open to every wind; and what a dazzling glare from the snow, for the view extended over twenty leagues of country. The whole of the little town of Phalsbourg, with its six bastions, its three demi-lunes, its two advanced posts, barracks, powder magazines, bridges, glacis and ramparts, its large *place d'armes*, and little houses in straight rows, all seemed as if drawn on white paper: one saw down to the bottom of the courts. Being unaccustomed to this sort of thing, I kept in the middle of the platform and dared not approach the clock, whose dial-plate is painted at the back with its hands, till Brainstein set me the example; then we set it by M. Goulden's great watch which I carried.

Then I looked towards Quatre Vents and recognized it and the house of my aunt Grédel. The chimney smoke ascended like a blue thread to the sky. I saw the kitchen again; I fancied Catherine in sabots and woollen petticoats, spinning in the fireside corner. Old Brainstein, who did not know what I was looking at, said, "Ay, Master Joseph, in spite of the snow, the roads are now all covered with people coming to learn the truth of their misfortune."

It was so; all the roads were covered with people who were coming into the town, and the *Place* was full of crowds standing before the *corps de garde* of the *mairie* and the post-office.

When, descending into the organ-loft, we saw the church also crowded with women on their knees, the thought for the first time occurred to me that if I had gone the year before, Catherine would have been there praying God for me. I felt myself shiver all over.

Brainstein went home, and I traversed the *Place* to go to M. le Commandant Meunier.

At the corner of the Hôtel de Ville, I saw more than five hundred persons standing before the great placard; townspeople and peasants, men and women, crowded together, all pale, with outstretched necks, gazing at it in silence as something terrible. From time to time they said to each other in German or French—

"But they can't all be dead! They will come back any way."

Others cried—"But one can't see—one can't get near!"

A poor old woman behind lifted her hands exclaiming—"Christopher! my poor Christopher!"

Others, as if provoked at hearing her, said—"Stop that old woman!"

Each thought only of himself.

At last, Harmentier, the *sergent de ville*, came out from the archway of the *corps de garde*, and placed himself at the top of the steps, with a placard exactly like that on the wall. This he began to read; it was called the twenty-ninth bulletin, and in it the Emperor related that during the retreat the horses perished every night by thousands. He said nothing about the men!

The *sergent de ville* read slowly: no one uttered a word. The old woman, who did not understand French, listened like the rest. One might have heard the buzzing of a fly. But when he came to this passage, "Our cavalry was so much dismounted that it was found necessary to unite all the officers who still had a horse remaining in order to form four companies of five hundred men each. The generals performed the functions of the captains, the colonels those of the subalterns."—when he read this passage, which told more of the misery of the great army than all the rest, cries and groans were heard on all sides, and two or three women fainted.

It is true the placard added, "The health of His Majesty has never been better," and this was a great consolation. Unhappily it could not restore to life the three hundred thousand men buried in the snow. So the people went very sadly away! Others who had heard nothing came by the dozen, and from hour to hour Harmentier came out to read the bulletin.

This lasted till the evening, and every time it was the same.

I went to M. le Commandant de Place. Entering the drawing-room, I found him at breakfast. He was an elderly man, but hearty, with red face and good appetite.

"Ah! it's you," he said: "M. Goulden isn't come?"

"No, Monsieur," I said, "the bad news has made him ill."

"Ah! well, well," he said, emptying his glass, "I can understand—yes, it's a sad case."

And while I lifted up the glass cover of the timepiece, he added—

"Bah! Tell M. Goulden that we shall have our revenge. One can't always be having the best of it—hang it! We've been regularly beating them for fifteen years: it's only fair to leave them this little rag of consolation. Besides, our honour is all safe: we have not been beaten: but for the snow and frost these poor Cossacks would have had hard lines. But a little patience—the lists will soon be filled up, and then! . . . ."

I set the timepiece: he rose and came to look on, having a great taste for clock-making. Then as I was about to retire, he cried cheerily, buttoning up again his great-coat which he had thrown open to eat at his ease—

"Tell old Goulden to be easy; the dance will begin again in the spring: they won't always be having the winter on their side, those Kalmucs!—tell him that!"

His large good-humoured face had a little consoled me; but in all the other houses to which I went, nothing but wailings were to be heard. The women especially were plunged in grief; the men said nothing, but walked up and down with sunken heads, not even looking at what I was doing.

About ten o'clock I had only two persons left to see—M. de la Vablerie Chamberlan, an old noble, who lived at the bottom of the High Street, with Madame Chamberlan d'Ecok, and Mademoiselle Jeanne, their daughter. These were emigrants who had come back three or four years ago. They visited nobody in the town, and saw only three or four old curés in the neighbourhood. M. de la Vablerie Chamberlan cared for nothing but hunting: he had six hounds in his yard, and a carriage and pair. One old man served them for coachman, groom, footman, and whipper-in. M. de la Vablerie always wore a hunting-coat, a leather cap and boots and spurs. All the town called him "old crackbrain;" but nothing was ever said about Madame or Mademoiselle Chamberlan.

I felt very sad as I pushed open the heavy swing door, that kept on a long rattling in the vestibule; but what was my surprise to hear, amidst this general desolation, the sound of singing to the harpsichord. M. de la Vablerie was singing and Mademoiselle Jeanne accompanied him. At that time I did not know that the misfortune of one was the good fortune of another; and I thought, with my hand on the latch, "They don't yet know the news from Russia."

Mdlle. Louise, the servant, let me in by the kitchen way, and shewed me into the large drawing-room, which was seldom entered; the *persiennes* of the lofty windows looking on the court were closed, but there was light enough for what I had to do. I regulated the old time-piece, a magnificent work in white marble, Mdlle. Louise looking on.

"Have you company, Mademoiselle Louise?" I said to her.

"No; but Monsieur gave me notice to let nobody in.'

"They are very merry here?"

"Ah, yes," she said, "it's the first time for years. I don't know what's taken them."

The idea never occurred to me that they were rejoicing over our defeat.

I then went to old Feral, who was called the "Standard-bearer," because at the age of forty-eight, being a smith and father of a family, he had carried the Phalsbourg Volunteers' colours in '92, and had not come back till after the campaign of Zurich. His three sons were in the Russian army—John, Louis, and George: George was a major in the dragoons, the two others were infantry officers.

I had imagined to myself beforehand the grief of old Feral, but it was nothing to what I saw on entering his room. The poor old man, bald and blind. sat in the armchair behind the stove, his head bent on his breast, and his large black eyes wide open, as if he had seen his three sons stretched at his feet. He said nothing; but large drops stood on his forehead and trickled down on his thin pale cheeks, and his face was so pale he seemed about to breathe his last. Four or five of his old comrades of the days of the Republic had come to console him. They sat around him in the greatest silence, smoking their pipes and wearing an air of deep dejection.

From time to time one or the other said—

"Come, come, Feral, are we no longer veterans of the army of Sambre and Meuse?"

Or, perhaps—

"Courage, Standard-bearer, courage! Why, didn't we storm the great battery of Fleurus at a run?"

But he made no answer; only from minute to minute he sighed, his old hollow cheeks swelled, then he bent down again: his comrades made signs to each other, shaking their heads as if to say, "A bad job."

When I returned I found M. Goulden at the counter.

"Well, Joseph?" he said.

"Well, Monsieur Goulden, you were right to stay away. It's terrible!"

And I told him all in detail.

"Yes, I knew that," he said mournfully; "but this is but the beginning of worse misfortunes. These Prussians, Austrians, Russians, Spaniards, and all the people whom we have pillaged since 1804, will profit by our misery to fall upon us. Since we wished to give them kings whom they did not know from Adam, and whom they did not want, they are going to do the like by us, with a train of nobles and all. So after having been bled to the last drop for the Emperor's brother, we shall lose all that we had gained by the Revolution. Instead of being the first, we shall be the very last and lowest. Yes, that is what is now to happen to us: since with us the soldiers were everything, and we have no more soldiers, now we are nothing!"

I laid the table, and whilst we sat silent at dinner, the church bells began to toll.

"Some one is dead in the town," said M. Goulden. Ten minutes after came in the rabbi Rose to have a glass put to his watch.

"Who is dead?" asked M. Goulden.

"The old Standard-bearer!"

"What! the good old Feral?"

"Yes, about twenty minutes since. Old Desmarets and several others tried to comfort him. At last he asked them to read to him his son George's last letter, the major of dragoons, telling him that next spring he hoped to embrace him in a colonel's epaulettes. Whilst listening to this he suddenly tried to rise, but fell back again with his head on his knees: that letter broke his heart!"

M. Goulden made no remark.

"There, M. Rose," he said, giving him his watch, "it's twelve sous."

We finished our dinner in silence.

CHAPTER V.

Some days after, the Gazette announced that the Emperor was in Paris, and that the King of Rome and the Empress Marie Louise were going to be crowned. The maire, the deputy, and the municipal councillors, spoke of nothing but the rights of the crown, and an express discourse even was delivered on it in the town-hall. But people were not much moved, because each one was afraid of being carried off by the conscription; and for my part, I fell away visibly. In vain did M. Goulden say to me, "Don't be afraid, Joseph; you could not march. Consider, my boy, a fellow as lame as you would be left behind at the first stage." I remained full of anxiety.

When we were at work alone, M. Goulden sometimes said to me—

"If those who are our masters, and who say God placed them on the earth for our good, could picture to themselves, at the beginning of a campaign, the poor old men, the sorrowing mothers, whose very hearts they tear out, as it were, to satisfy their pride—if they could witness their tears and groans at the moment when it is announced to them, 'Your child is dead!—you will never see him more: he perished under the horses' hoofs, or was struck down by a bullet, or lay in a hospital far off, after being amputated, in a fever, with no one to comfort him, calling for you as when he was a little child!'—if they could picture it to themselves, I think there is not one barbarous enough to go on. But they think of nothing; they think others don't love their children as much as *they* do theirs: they take the people for brute beasts! They are mistaken: all their great genius and their great ideas of glory are nothing. There is but one thing for which a nation ought to go to war—men, women, children, old men—that is, when our liberty is attacked as it was in '92; then all die or win together: he who remains behind is a coward, who expects others to fight for him; the victory is not for some but for all; the son and father defend their family; if they are killed 'tis a misfortune, but they die for their rights. That, Joseph, is the only just war, where nobody can complain; all the others are shameful, and the glory they bring is not that of a man, but of a savage beast!"

Suddenly, on the 8th of January, a great placard was stuck up against the *mairie*, telling us that the Emperor was going, by a Senatus-consultus as it was called then, to make a levy first of 150,000 conscripts of 1813; then of 100 cohorts of 1812, who imagined themselves to have got off; afterwards 100,000 conscripts of from 1809 to 1812, and so on to the end; thus all the gaps would be filled up, and we should have even a larger army than before to go to Russia.

On reading this placard I almost fainted; nor was I the only one thus affected. In this year many young men refused to go: some broke their teeth to hinder themselves from being able to bite cartridges, others shot off their thumbs with pistols, others fled to the woods: they were called refractory, and *gendarmes* enough could not be found to run after them. At the same time mothers of families took courage, in a manner, to rebel, and to encourage their boys not to obey the *gendarmes*. They helped them in every way; they cried out against the Emperor, and the curés supported them: in a word, the measure was full!

That very day I went to Quatre Vents; but it was not in the joy of my heart, but as one who is being despoiled of his love and his life. I knew not how to announce our misfortune, and on entering I saw they knew it already, for Catherine was weeping bitterly and Aunt Grédel was pale with indignation.

The first word my aunt said to me, while pushing fiercely her grey hairs back behind her ears, was—

"You shan't go! What do his wars matter to us? The curé himself said it was too much; that we ought to make peace. Don't cry, Catherine; I tell you he *shall* stay!"

Then, all livid with anger, knocking her saucepans about, she went on—

"It's ever so long that all this carnage has disgusted me; first of all our two poor cousins Kasper and Yokel must needs have their bones broken in Spain for this Emperor of ours, and now he comes again to ask for our young men: he is not content with having caused the death of three hundred thousand in Russia. We shall see! we shall see!"

"For heaven's sake hush, Aunt Grédel!" I said, looking towards the window; "you may be heard and we shall all be ruined!"

"Why, I speak to be heard," she said; "I'm not afraid of your Napoleon: he began with stopping us from speaking, so that he might do whatever he pleased; but that's all coming to an end! This man has no heart; he will come to a bad end! God has shown himself this winter: he saw that we had more fear of a man than of him; that even the mothers dared not keep back their own flesh, when he required it to be massacred; so he made the cold come, and our army perished, and all who are to go are dead beforehand: God is weary of it! As for you, you shan't go," she added resolutely; "you shall escape into the woods with Jean Krap, Louis Bême, and all the stoutest young fellows here; you will go over the mountains into Switzerland, and Catherine and I will go to join you, till the end of this extermination."

Then Aunt Grédel stopped speaking. Instead of giving us the ordinary dinner, she gave us a still better one than the Sunday before, saying to us in a firm tone—

"Eat, my children: don't be afraid; all this will be altered."

At four o'clock in the afternoon I returned to Phalsbourg, somewhat calmer than before. But as I ascended the Rue de la Munitionnaire, what should I hear but the drum of the *sergent-de-ville* Harmentier, with a great crowd around him. I ran to hear the announcements and came just as they began.

Harmentier read aloud that, by the Senatus-consultus of the 3rd, the drawing for recruits would be on the 15th.

This was the 8th, so that only seven days remained to us. All dispersed in silence, and I returned sorrowfully to M. Goulden.

My grief on that and the following days may be imagined. I could not keep in one place, and every moment I was on the point of abandoning the country. I fancied myself already running through the woods, with gendarmes on my track, crying, "Stop! stop!" Then I thought of the wretchedness of Catherine, Aunt Grédel, and M. Goulden. Sometimes I fancied myself marching in rank with a number of other wretches, with "Forward! With the bayonet!" sounding in our ears, while bullets were sweeping down whole files: I seemed to hear the bullets and cannon-balls whistling. I was in a pitiable condition.

"Be calm, Joseph," said M. Goulden; "don't torment yourself so. Think that of all the conscription there are not perhaps ten who can give such good reasons as you for staying at home. The sergeant must be blind if he takes you. Besides, I shall see the commandant of the place. Be calm!"

Still, when the day for the drawing came, I looked so pale and miserable that the parents of conscripts seemed in a manner to envy my looks, thinking of their sons. "He," they said, "is in luck; a breath would blow him away. Some people are born under a lucky star!"

CHAPTER VI.

The town-hall of Phalsbourg was worth seeing on the morning of the 15th January, during the drawing for the conscription. Even now, it is something serious to be taken and forced to leave one's parents, friends, villages, one's earth and one's land, to go, Heaven knows where! But one comes back in seven years: one can say with some confidence, "In seven years, I shall find my old home again, my parents, perhaps my sweetheart. I shall have seen the world. I shall even have a claim to be *garde forestière*." But at that time, if you had the misfortune to lose, all was over. Then not one out of a hundred came back; the idea of having definitively to go off *could* not enter your head.

That day, then, those of Hasberg, Gasbourg, and Quatre Vents, were to draw first; afterwards those of the town; lastly, those of Wechem and Mittelbronn.

I got up early, and with my two elbows on the counter I set myself to watching all those people pass:

those lads in blouses, those poor old men in nightcaps and jackets, those old women in bedgown and woollen skirt, with bent backs and dejected faces, with stick or umbrella under their arm. They went in families. M. the *sous-préfet* of Sambourg, in a silver-embroidered collar, and his secretary, were also looking out from the windows of the "Bœuf Rouge."

The drawing began at 9 o'clock, and ere long clarionet and violin were heard in the streets playing the "Swedish March." To this air thousands of poor wretches have quitted Alsace for ever. The recruits danced, swung about arm-in-arm, rent the air with their shouts and stamped on the ground while waving their hats, trying to seem joyous with despair in their hearts. Such was the fashion.

I was just going out when Aunt Grédel and Catherine entered, saying—

"Good morning, M. Goulden! we are come on account of the conscription."

I saw at once by Catherine's red eyes how much she had been weeping.

M. Goulden said to them—

"It will soon be the time for the young men of the town?"

"Yes, M. Goulden," answered Catherine faintly, "those of Hasberg have finished."

"Well, well," said he, "Joseph, 'tis time for you to go. But don't be vexed nor frightened. These drawings, you see, are nothing but forms where nobody ever wins; or if they do, they are caught again in a year or two later. But when the revising council assembles, we shall see what's best to be done."

Then I went out with Catherine and her aunt, and we walked to the great Place, where the crowd was collected. In all the shops, dozens of recruits, going to buy ribbons, jostled each other round the counters, weeping and singing at once, like creatures possessed.

In front of the *corps-de-garde* I perceived a good way off the hawker Pinacle, his pack open on a little table, and on one side a tall pole adorned with ribbons, which he sold to the conscripts. I was hastening by, when he called out—

"Here, cripple, stop! Come here. I am keeping a fine ribbon for you: you ought to have a magnificent one—the conqueror's ribbon!"

He held above his head a great black ribbon, and I turned pale in spite of myself. But as we ascended the steps of the mairie, just then there came down them a conscript: it was Klipfel, the smith of the French Gate. He had just drawn number 8, and cried out—

"The black ribbon, Pinacle—the black ribbon! Let's have it—whatever it costs!"

He looked gloomy, but laughed. His little brother Jean was behind weeping, and cried, "No, Jacob, no; not the black ribbon!"

But Pinacle had already fastened the black ribbon on to the smith's hat, the latter saying, "That's what we require now. We are all dead—we must wear mourning for ourselves!"

And with a savage voice he cried, "*Vive l'Empereur!*" I glided quickly through the crowd to escape Pinacle.

We had no end of trouble in entering under the archway of the *mairie* and climbing the old oak staircase, where people were swarming up and down like ants. In the great hall above, the gendarme walked about slowly, maintaining order as much as possible. And in the council-room at the side the numbers were being called, while from time to time a conscript came forth, with his face violently flushed, fixing his number to his cap, and going out with head down through the crowd, like a mad bull blind with rage and ready to break his horns against the walls. Others, on the contrary, passed along pale as corpses. The windows of the *mairie* were open; five or six bands of music were playing outside. It was frightful.

In the hall we saw M. the *sous-préfet*, with the mayors and secretaries on their tribune, calling the numbers aloud as though pronouncing judgment; for all those numbers were in truth sentences of doom.

We waited a long time; I had not a drop of blood in my veins, when at last my name was called. I came forward without seeing or hearing; I put my hand in the box and drew out a number.

M. the *sous-préfet* called "Number 17!"

I said nothing, and went away, Catherine and her aunt following me. When I had got into the air, I remembered that I had drawn number 17. Aunt Grédel appeared confounded, Catherine was deadly pale; and so we returned to M. Goulden's house.

When he heard the number, he appeared troubled, but said presently—

"As well that as another—all must go—the lists must be filled up. But that won't concern Joseph. I shall go and see M. the commandant and M. the mayor.

It won't be telling them a lie to say that Joseph is lame: all the town knows it; but in the crowd it might be passed over. That's why I shall go to see them. So don't trouble yourselves: take heart."

These words reassured Aunt Grédel and Catherine, who returned to Quatre Vents, full of hope. But it was not so with me. From that moment I had not a minute's peace of mind by day or by night.

The Emperor had one good habit—he did not leave the recruits long in suspense at their own homes. He was not like those tooth-drawers who show you first their hooks and pincers, and look in your mouth long enough to set you shaking before they have made up their minds—he went to work at once! Immediately after the drawing, the council of revision arrived, and some days after, came the route.

A week after the drawing, the council of revision sat at the Hôtel de Ville, with all the mayors of the country and some notables. The day before, M. Goulden had gone to set the clocks of the mayor and commandant; he came back with a smiling face, and said to me—

"It will all be right. These gentlemen know very well that you are lame; they answered me at once—

'Why, M. Goulden, this young man is lame; what's the use of speaking to us about *him!* Don't disturb yourself: it isn't infirm people we want, but soldiers.'

These words fell like balm on my soul, and that night I slept the sleep of the blessed. But next day fear again seized on me; I bethought myself how many men with all kinds of defects went notwithstanding, and how many others were unscrupulous enough to invent them on purpose: for instance, swallowing hurtful things in order to make themselves pale, or tying a leg to produce a varicose vein, or pretending to be deaf, blind, or imbecile. Thinking of these things, I trembled lest I should not be considered lame enough, so I resolved to look like an invalid. I had heard say that vinegar produces pains in the stomach, and without telling M. Goulden, in my fright I swallowed all the vinegar that was in the little cruet. Then I dressed, thinking to look like a corpse dug up; for the vinegar was very strong, and made me feel very ill. But when I entered M. Goulden's room, he had scarcely looked at me before he cried out, "Why, Joseph, what's the matter with you? You are as red as a turkey-cock."

And I myself, looking in the glass, saw that my face was red up to the ears and the tip of the nose. Then, indeed, I was frightened; but instead of growing pale, I became still redder, and I cried out in my despair, "I am ruined now! I shall be looking like a fellow without any defect, and even in very good health: it's that vinegar that has got into my head."

"What vinegar?" asked M. Goulden.

"Why, from the cruet-stand, which I drank to make myself pale; as they say Mademoiselle Sclapp, the organist, did. O God! what an unlucky idea it was!"

"It won't prevent you from being lame," said M. Goulden. "Only you wanted to deceive the council, and that wasn't honest. But there's half-past nine striking; Werner has been here yesterday to let me know you would have to go before it at ten o'clock, so make haste."

I was forced, then, to set off in this state—my cheeks all in a blaze with the vinegar. When I fell in with my aunt and Catherine, who were waiting for me under the archway of the mairie, they scarcely knew me again.

"How pleased and happy you look!" said my aunt Grédel.

When I heard that, I should certainly have gone faint, but that the vinegar kept me up in spite of myself. I went up the stairs then, in a state of extreme distress, unable to utter a syllable, so enraged was I with my own stupidity.

At the top there were more than twenty-five poor fellows, who, though they had tried to pass themselves off as unsound, had already been received as conscripts; and more than twenty-five others, seated on a bench against the wall, were waiting their turn, with eyes fixed on the ground and rueful countenances.

The old gendarme Kelz in his great cocked hat was walking backwards and forwards; as soon as he saw me he stopped in surprise, then he cried out,—

"That's right! That's right! Here's one at least who isn't sorry to be off. One can see the longing for glory in his eyes!"

And placing his hand on my shoulder—"'Tis well, Joseph," said he; "I prophesy you will be a corporal at the end of the campaign."

"But I am lame," I cried, angrily.

"Lame," said Kelz, with a wink and a smile; "never mind; with such looks as those, one's sure to get on."

He had scarcely done speaking, when the council hall-door opened, and the other gendarme, Werner, appeared there and called out,—

"Joseph Bertha!"

I entered, limping as much as I could, and Werner reclosed the door. The mayors of the canton, the *sous-préfet*, the mayor of Phalsbourg and his secretary, were all there. A conscript of Hasberg was putting on his coat again; this man, with his long hair hanging over his eyes, bare neck, and mouth opened in a sigh, looked like a man going to be hung. Two doctors were there. At their direction I prepared myself for the usual medical inspection, and the *sous-préfet* said,—

"There's a healthy fellow for you!"

I rejoined politely,—

"But I am lame, M. le *sous-préfet*!"

The surgeons looked at me, and one of them, to whom the commandant had doubtless spoken of me, said,—

"The left leg is rather short."

"Bah!" said the other, "it's sound."

Then putting his hand on my chest, he said,—

"There's a healthy conformation: Cough."

I coughed as feebly as I could; but all the same, he declared I had good lungs, and added,—

"Look at his colour—that's good blood."

I put in anxiously, "I've been drinking vinegar."

"Ah! that proves you have a strong stomach," said he, "since you like vinegar."

"All that," said the mayor, "does not hinder this young man's being lame from his birth: it's a fact known to all Phalsbourg."

"Without doubt," said the hospital-surgeon, "it's a case for exemption."

"Yes," replied the mayor; "I am sure that this young man could not support a long march: he would be left behind at the second halting-place."

I thought myself saved, when the *sous-préfet* asked me,—"You are Joseph Bertha, are you not?"

On my assenting, he drew from his portfolio a letter, which he read aloud, recounting how, six months before, I had made a bet that I would go to Saverne and come back quicker than Pinacle; that we had run together in less than three hours, and that I had won.

Unhappily it was true! That wretched Pinacle had always called me lame, and in my anger I had made this bet with him. All the world knew of it; I could not assert the contrary.

"That settles the question," said the first surgeon; and turning to the secretary, exclaimed—"Fit for service!"

I turned away in despair; some one helped me to the stairs, where Catherine met me, and asked me what had passed: I should have fallen from the top to the bottom had not Aunt Grédel held me up. When we were out on the Place, I cried like a child, and Catherine also.

Aunt Grédel exclaimed, "Ah! the brigands! . . . now they are carrying off even the lame, and the infirm. They *must* have everything! Well then, let them come and take us too!"

People clustered together, and the butcher Lepel, while chopping his meat there on the block, said,—

"Mother Grédel, in Heaven's name, hold your tongue . . . . They wouldn't scruple to send you to prison."

"Let them send me there!" cried she, "let them massacre me! I say these men are cowards to permit such horrors!"

But the *sergent de ville* approaching, we went back again together weeping. We turned the corner of the Café Hemmerlé, and we went in to the house. People watched us from their windows and said, "There's another going!" M. Goulden, knowing that Aunt Grédel and Catherine were coming to dine with us on the day of the revision, had ordered from the *Mouton d'Or* a goose and two bottles of good Alsace wine. He was convinced then that I was going to be let off, and was surprised at our looks of despair.

"What is the matter?" he asked, gazing at us with wide open eyes.

Aunt Grédel answered: "The rascals have taken him!"

"It can't be!" said M. Goulden.

"Yes," said my aunt, "it's the greatest possible wickedness. Will there never be another revolution? Will these brigands always be masters?"

"Come, come, Mother Grédel, calm yourself," said M. Goulden; "in the name of Heaven, don't scream so. Joseph, tell it to us in a rational manner; they are mistaken—it must be so . . . . Didn't the mayor and the hospital-doctor say anything?"

With many a groan I told the story of the letter; and Aunt Grédel, who knew nothing about it, began to exclaim with clenched fists,—

"The brigand! if he will but come to us, I'll split his head with my hatchet."

M. Goulden was in consternation. "How! Didn't you cry out that it was false? Was that story, then, true?"

I hung my head in silence; and he added,—

"Ah, youth, youth! always thoughtless! What imprudence, what imprudence!"

He walked sorrowfully about the room, then sat down and wiped his spectacles, while Aunt Grédel said,—

"Yes! but they won't have him nevertheless; this evening Joseph will be in the mountains, on his way to Switzerland."

M. Goulden became grave, and replied after an instant,—

"'Tis a misfortune, a great misfortune; for Joseph is really lame: they will find that out before long. But you are wrong, Mother Grédel, in giving him bad counsel."

"Bad counsel!" she cried: "So you, too, are for having people massacred?"

"No," he said, "I do not love wars, especially those in which hundreds of thousands of men lose their lives for the glory of one alone. But those wars are done with. It is no longer to gain glory and kingdoms that soldiers are hired: it is to defend our country, compromised by tyranny and ambition. Peace is really desired *now!* Unhappily, the Russians advance, the Prussians are with them, and our friends the Austrians

5

are only waiting for a good opportunity to fall upon us. If we don't go to meet them, they will come to us. It's quite another thing, then, from our wars of Spain, Russia, and Germany. As for me, old as I am, Mother Grédel, if the danger continues to increase, and if the old Republicans are wanted, I should be ashamed to go and make clocks in Switzerland while others shed their blood in defence of their country. Besides, listen to this—deserters are everywhere despised. After having taken such a step, one has ties nowhere—no longer father, mother, village, or country. One has adjudged oneself incapable of fulfilling the first of one's duties, which is to love and maintain one's country, even when it is in the wrong."

Aunt Grédel persisted, and I said at last—

"Listen, Aunt Grédel. You know I love nothing so much as peace and tranquillity; but I should not wish to escape like a vagabond into other countries. Still I will do what Catherine wishes. If she tells me to go into Switzerland, I *will* go."

Then Catherine, dropping her head to hide her tears, said in a very low voice,—

"I should not like people to be able to call you a deserter."

"Well, then," I cried, "I will do as the rest! Since the Phalsbourg and Dalsberg people go to the war, I will go!"

M. Goulden observed, "Every one is free to choose; but I am glad to see that Joseph thinks as I do."

When they took their leave, Catherine, falling on my neck, wept so that M. Goulden could not refrain from tears; and as for me, when I shut the door behind them, I was so unhappy that I can scarcely bear to think of it even now.

CHAPTER VII.

From that day I had no head for anything: I tried at first to return to my work, but my thoughts were always elsewhere. M. Goulden himself said—

"Never mind, Joseph; make use of the time which remains to you with us. Go and see Catherine and Mother Grédel. I still think you will be invalided—but who knows?"

So every morning I went to Quatre Vents, and passed my days with Catherine. We were very sad, and yet very happy to be together. We loved each other, if possible, more than before.

At night, between eight and nine o'clock, I returned, just when they shut the gates, and in passing I saw all the little inns full of conscripts and old invalided soldiers, who were drinking together. The conscripts always paid; the others, with their greasy forage-caps over one ear and red noses, curled up their moustaches whilst telling with majestic air of their battles, marches, and duels.

Nothing could be more abominable than the sight of these holes full of smoke, with lamps suspended under the gloomy beams, these old campaigners and young fellows, hard at work drinking, shouting, and rapping the tables, while behind, in the shade, sate some old Annette Schnaps or Marie Hering, her old wig at the back of her head and her comb with three crooked teeth, looking on, scratching her head, or emptying a jug to the health of the fine fellows.

It was sad that the sons of peasants, honest laborious fellows, should lead such a life; but no one any longer wished to work: they would have given their lives for twopence. What with shouting, drinking, and cursing their lot, they finished by falling asleep with their heads on the table, while the old ones emptied the jugs, singing—

"Glory calls us!"

Seeing these things, I blessed Heaven in my misery for giving me good honest friends to sustain my courage and keep me from falling into such hands.

This went on till the 25th of January. For some days before a great number of Italian conscripts,

Piedmontese and Genoese, had been arriving in the town. The former, fat and robust, like Savoyards, fed on chestnuts, with great pointed hats on their curly heads, drugget trousers of dull green colour, and short jackets, also of drugget, but brick-coloured, fastened by a leathern belt: they had enormous shoes, and ate cheese on their thumbs, seated all along the old market-place. The others, dry, thin, and brown, shivered in their long ragged coats merely at seeing the snow on the roof, and looked at the women who passed with large, black, melancholy eyes. They were daily drilled on the *Place*, for they were to be drafted into the 6th regiment of the line at Mayence, and were only stopping a little while in the infantry barracks.

The captain of recruits, who was called Vidal, lodged over our chamber. He was a square, stout, firm man, and also very kindly and honest. When he knew that I was a conscript, and was afraid of not coming back, he encouraged me, saying, "It's all habit: at the end of five or six months one marches and fights just as one eats one's supper; and many get so accustomed to firing at others, that they consider themselves ill off when they have not that enjoyment."

But his way of reasoning was not to my taste; the

more so that I saw on one of his cheeks five or six grains of powder which had gone very deep below the skin : this he explained had been the effect of a musket-shot discharged by a Russian almost under his nose. The prospect saddened me more and more; but as several days passed without news, I began to think that I had been forgotten, like Jacob of the *Chévrehof*, of whom people speak even now on account of his extraordinary good luck.

However, on the morning of the 25th, just as I was going to start for Quatre Vents, M. Goulden turned to me and said,—

"Look here, Joseph: I wished to let you sleep in peace one night more; but—after all, you *must* know it, my boy—last night, the brigadier of the gendarmes came to bring me the route for you. You go with the Piedmontese and Genoese, and five or six of the town lads, to Mayence."

I sat down, unable to speak a word. M. Goulden began slowly to read the route; all that I remember is that Joseph Bertha, native of Dabo, canton of Phalsbourg, *arrondissement* of Sarrebourg, was incorporated in the 6th regiment of the line, and was to join his corps on the 29th January at Mayence.

After an instant's silence, M. Goulden added, "The Italians leave to-day about eleven o'clock."

Then, as if awakening from a bad dream, I cried—

"But shall I then see Catherine no more?"

"Yes, Joseph, yes," he said, in a faltering voice: "I have had them told; they will come, and you will embrace them before starting."

Again he went on,—"You needn't trouble yourself about anything; I have prepared all beforehand. And when you come back, Joseph, if God should spare me for so long, you will find me always the same. My greatest happiness would have been to have you as a son, for I have always found in you a good heart and a good head. I would have made over my stock to you: Catherine and you would have been my children. . . . But we must be resigned: and all this is but for a little while—I am quite sure you will be sent back, for they will soon see that you cannot make long marches."

He laid on the table a soldier's knapsack, observing, "There's your kit; I have put inside all you will want, cotton and flannel shirts, and the rest. I have had shoes made for you, for nothing can be worse than the shoes of the contractors: they are almost always of horse's skin, and heat the feet terribly. You are not too strong on your legs, my poor boy. Well—that's all." And he sat down.

Outside you could hear the bustle of the Italians who were preparing to start. Overhead Captain Vidal was giving orders. All this noise and movement produced a strange effect on me, and while yet bewildered with it, I saw the door open, and Catherine threw herself sobbing into my arms.

Whilst Aunt Grédel cried out,—

"Didn't I tell you you ought to escape to Switzerland, and that these rascals would end by carrying you off? Didn't I tell you? And you wouldn't believe me."

"Aunt Grédel," replied M. Goulden immediately, "To depart when our duty requires us, is not so great a misfortune as to be despised by all honest men. These cries and reproaches do no good: you would be better employed in comforting and supporting Joseph."

"Ah!" said she, "I don't reproach him! No indeed! Though it's dreadful to see things like these."

Catherine never left me; she sat beside me, and we kissed each other. "You will return?" she said, pressing me to her.

"Yes, yes," I said to her in a low voice. "And

you—you must always think of me—you must never love another."

"Oh no," she sobbed out, "I will never love any one but you."

I could only attend to Catherine: we sat side by side embracing each other. This lasted about a quarter of an hour, when Captain Vidal entered, with his cloak rolled over his shoulder.

"Well!" said he; "well! And our young man?"

"There he is," said M. Goulden.

"Ah, yes; they're going to break their hearts about it—that's natural enough. I remember that myself: we all leave some one behind."

Then raising his voice—"Come, young man, courage! We are no longer a child, hang it!"

He looked at Catherine. "Nevertheless," he said, "I understand his not liking to go."

The drums were beating at all the street-corners; the captain added,—

"We have still twenty minutes before starting;" and glancing at me, saying, "Don't miss the first roll-call, young man," he pressed M. Goulden's hand, and was gone.

I could not let Catherine go. But suddenly the roll

of drums began. All were now collected on the Place. M. Goulden took my knapsack from the table by its straps, saying in a grave voice,—

" Joseph, bid us adieu : it is time."

I rose up all pale. He fastened the knapsack to my shoulders. Catherine sat sobbing, with her face in her hands. Aunt Grédel stood looking at me with lips compressed. The roll of drums went on still: suddenly it stopped.

" The roll-call is going to begin," said M. Goulden, embracing me ; suddenly he burst into tears, called me his child, and whispered—" Courage ! "

Aunt Grédel embraced me with violent outcries of grief. I could weep no more. I approached Catherine, who did not stir, and kissed her neck. Still she did not rise, and I went away very quickly ; for all my strength was gone, when she began with a heart-rending voice to cry out,—" Joseph ! Joseph ! "

I turned ; we threw ourselves into each other's arms, and remained there some instants, sobbing. I replaced the fainting Catherine in the chair, and went out without daring to turn my head.

I was already on the *Place*, when the drums began again : then I saw that I was between Klipfel and Fürst, both with their knapsacks on their backs; their parents were there, weeping as at a funeral. Near the Hôtel de Ville was Captain Vidal on his little grey horse, talking with two officers. The sergeants began the roll-call, and each one answered to his name. Then the captain cried, "March!" and we went two and two towards the French gate.

At the corner, by Spitz, the baker's, an old woman on the first floor cried from her window with a choking voice—

"Kasper! Kasper!"

It was Zébédé's grandmother. Zébédé raised his hand without replying; he too was very sad, and hung down his head. I trembled at the thought of passing my own home. When we reached it I heard a cry from the windows; but I turned my head to the "Bœuf Rouge" opposite, and the noise of the drums drowned all besides.

The children ran after us crying,—"There they are, going away. Look! there's Klipfel, there's Joseph!"

We passed through the French gate, traversed the advanced post, where the drums ceased, turned to the right, and had already passed the farm of Gerberhoff, and were about to descend to the great bridge, when I heard some one speak to me. It was the captain, who cried from his saddle,—

"Well done, young man: I am pleased with you!"

At this I could not help again shedding tears: nor could Fürst either, big as he was; the others were pale as death, but said nothing. On the bridge Zébédé took out his pipe to smoke. The Italians talked and laughed among themselves, having had three weeks to accustom themselves to this life.

Once on the road to Metting, at about a league from the town, just as we were going down hill, Klipfel touched my shoulder, and turning his head, said—

"Look down there."

I looked, and saw Phalsbourg far beneath us, the barracks, powder magazines, and the steeple from which I had seen Catherine's house six weeks before, all grey, and the woods black around it. Gladly would I have stopped there a few minutes; but the troop moved on, and I with it. We went down hill to Metting.

CHAPTER VIII.

The same day we went as far as Biche; next day, to Hombach; next day to Kaiserslautern, &c. The weather had become snowy again.

We traversed numberless villages, sometimes in the mountains, sometimes in the plain. On entering every market town, the drums beat a march, and we held up our heads and stepped out in time, to give ourselves the air of old soldiers. The people came to their windows or doors saying,—"They're conscripts!"

At the evening halt we were happy to rest our wearied feet, and none more than I. I cannot say that my leg hurt me; but my feet—Ah! I had never felt such fatigue! With our billets we had the right to a seat in the chimney-corner; but the people gave us a place at their tables as well. Almost always we had potatoes; sometimes also fresh bacon frizzling on a plate of sauerkraut. The children came to see us;

the old women asked us what country we were of, and what we did before we left; the young girls looked sadly at us, thinking of their lovers, who were gone five, six, or seven months before. Then I was taken to the boys' bed; with what joy I stretched myself in it! How I longed to sleep there twelve good hours! But early, at daybreak, the rolling of the drum awoke me; I looked at the dusky beams of the ceiling, the small frost-covered panes, and asked myself,—"Where am I?" And my heart sank as I said to myself, "At Biche, at Kaiserslautern. I am a conscript!" And I had to get dressed quickly, resume my knapsack, and hasten to answer to the roll-call.

"A good journey to you!" the housewife, thus early roused up, would say.

"Thank'e," answered the conscript, and was gone.

Aye truly, "a good journey!" You will never be seen again, poor fellow! How many others have followed the same road!

I shall never forget how at Kaiserslautern, the second day after our departure, having unbuckled my knapsack to get out a clean shirt, I discovered under the linen a small but rather heavy packet; on opening it, I found there fifty-four francs, in six-livre pieces, and on the paper these words of M. Goulden's,—"Be always honest and kindhearted in war. Think of all those for whom you would give your life, and treat foreigners humanely, that they may do the same in their turn. And may Heaven guide and guard you. Here is some money, Joseph. It is good, when away from one's friends, always to have a little money. Write to us as often as you can. I embrace you tenderly, my son."

Reading this I was much moved, and said to myself —"I am not entirely forsaken: good people are thinking of me! Never will I forget their good counsels!"

At last, on the fifth day, about ten o'clock in the evening, we entered Mayence. It was terribly cold; we had started early, and long before arriving at the town we had traversed villages full of soldiers, cavalry and infantry; dragoons in short jackets with *sabots* full of straw were going to break the ice in troughs to water their horses, others dragged trusses of fodder to the stable doors; there were also convoys of powder and shot, all white with frost; expresses; detachments of artillery; pontoniers, going and coming over the whitened region, and paying us no more attention than if we did not exist.

Captain Vidal, to warm himself, had dismounted and

was walking stoutly on; the officers and sergeants hurried us on, as we were late. Five or six Italians had remained behind in the villages, unable to advance. My feet were burning hot with pain, and at the last halt I could scarcely start again. The other Phalsbourgians walked well.

Night had come on; all were on the watch, and we said to ourselves, "We are near!" for on the horizon a dark line with black points and sparkling spires announced a great town.

At last we entered the advanced posts, across the zigzag earthworks. At the corner of a species of *demi-lune* we saw the city-moat full of ice, the ramparts of brick at the top, and fronting us, an old gloomy gate, with the drawbridge raised. Above, a sentinel presenting his musket, cried out—

"Who goes there?"

The captain, in advance by himself, cried—

"France!"

"What regiment?"

"Recruits of the 6th foot!"

Then a great silence. The drawbridge fell, and the guard came to reconnoitre: one of them carried a great lantern. Captain Vidal went a few steps in advance to speak with the commandant; we were then allowed to enter. We traversed a wide bridge, passed through a second gate resembling the first, and were in the city, which is paved with large stones. Each did his best not to limp, for, though it was night, all the inns and the shops were open, their large windows glittering, and hundreds of people came and went as in broad day.

We soon arrived at a small *Place*, and before a lofty barrack "Halt!" was called. There was an archway at the corner of it, and under this archway sat a *cantinière* behind a little table, under a great tricolor umbrella from which hung two lanterns.

Almost immediately several officers arrived; these were the commandant Gemeau and others whom I have since known. They shook hands, laughing, with our captain; then looked at us, and the roll was called. After that we received each a loaf of ammunition bread, and a billet for our quarters. We were warned that we should be called over next morning at eight o'clock, for the distribution of arms; the order "Break your ranks!" was given, and the officers went together into a large café. But we! where should we go with our billets, in the midst of a city like that? especially the Italians, who did not know a word of German or French?

My first idea was to go and see the *cantinière* under her umbrella. She was an old Alsatian, plump, and rosy-cheeked, who when I asked her where the *Capougner Strasse* was, answered—

"What are you going to spend?"

I was obliged to take a glass of brandy with her, and then she said—

"There, just in front of us, turning the corner to the right—there is the *Capougner Strasse*. Good-night, conscript!"

Fürst and Zébédé had their billets for the same street, so we three went off together, and Fürst found his house first. Whilst he was knocking, I discovered mine, for there was light in the two windows; I pushed open the door and came into a narrow passage, where I smelt new bread, to my great inward delight. Zébédé went on further; I called out in the passage, "No one there?"

Almost immediately an old woman appeared, with her candle, at the top of a wooden staircase. I showed my billet, and she said in German, "Come!"

I went upstairs, and passing, saw through an open door two men at work, naked to the waist.

I was at a baker's: no doubt the old woman worked too, which was why she was still up. She seemed melancholy. She led me to a good-sized room, with a porcelain stove, and a bed at the further end.

"You come late," she observed.

"Yes, we have been marching all day," I answered, scarcely able to speak; "and I am sinking with hunger and fatigue."

She looked at me and said, "Poor boy! poor boy!"

Then she made me sit by the stove, and asked me—

"Do your feet hurt you?"

"Yes, these three days."

"Well," she said, "take off your shoes and put on these *sabots;* I am coming back."

She left her candle on the table and went down again. I took off my knapsack and my shoes; my feet were blistered, and I thought, "My God! my God! can one suffer so much? Would it not be better to be dead?"

This idea had occurred to me a hundred times on the way; and now, beside this good fire, I felt myself so weary, so unhappy, that I should have liked to go to sleep for ever: notwithstanding Catherine, Aunt Grédel, M. Goulden, and all who wished me well.

The door opened, and there entered a tall, strong man, with a grey head: one of those I had seen below. He now had a shirt on, and carried a jug and two glasses. The old woman came in behind him with a wooden bowl which she set on the ground beside me.

"Take a foot-bath," she said, "it will do you good."

I was moved, and thought to myself, "Well, there are kind people in the world!" The blisters were bleeding, and the old woman repeated, "Poor boy! poor boy!"

The man said to her, "Go and fetch one of our *galettes*. This young man will take a glass of wine, and then we will let him sleep in peace."

He pushed the table before me, filled our glasses with an excellent white wine, and drank to my health. The wife re-entered with a large *galette*, all hot and covered with fresh, half-melted butter. I then first felt how hungry I was; but the good woman told me first to take my feet out of the water, and bending, she dried them herself with her apron before I knew what she was going to do. Then I exclaimed,—

"Oh, madame, you treat me as if I were your child!"

She paused a moment, and then said—

"We have a son in the army!"

I heard her voice tremble, and my heart bled.

"Eat and drink," said the man, cutting up the cake. I obeyed with a feeling of enjoyment I had never known before. Both watched me gravely, and when I had done, the man said—

"Yes, we have a son in the army. He went last year to Russia, and we have had no news of him . . . . These wars are terrible!"

He saw my eyes closing, and said suddenly, "Well, good night!" As they both went out I cried, "Thank you, and may God bring you back your son!"

Then I undressed, got into bed, and slept profoundly.

CHAPTER IX.

NEXT morning I awoke about seven o'clock. A trumpet was sounding to arms in the *Capougner Strasse.* Everything was astir; horses, carriages, and people passed. My feet still hurt me a little; but it was nothing compared with what it had been. When I had put on clean stockings I felt as if new-made; I was firm on my legs, and said to myself, "If this lasts I shall become a stout fellow: it's only the beginning."

I dressed in this cheerful mood. The baker's wife had set my shoes by the stove to dry, after having filled them with hot ashes to keep them from hardening, and they were well blacked and polished. I buckled on my knapsack and went down, without having had time to thank my kind hosts; but thinking to perform this duty after the roll-call.

Along one whole side of the *Place* were ranged cannons mounted on carriages. Horses arrived from their watering places, led by Baden hussars: some artillerymen and dragoons were among the number. In front of us was a cavalry barrack, and on the other three sides of the *Place* were old houses with gables and carved figures as at Saverne, only much larger: never did I see anything like it. As I was staring at the scene the drums began to beat, and all fell into rank. Captain Vidal appeared, and it was announced, first in Italian, then in French, that the arms were going to be given out, and each one was to step out of the ranks as his name was called.

The carriages stopped ten paces off, and the roll-call began. Each in his turn stepped out of the ranks and received a cartridge-box, a sword, a bayonet, and a musket. These were belted over the blouse, the coat, or the cloak; and we looked, with our hats, caps, and arms, like a veritable band of brigands. I received a musket so large and heavy that I could scarcely carry it, and as the cartridge-box hung down almost to my calves, Sergeant Pinto showed me the way to shorten the straps. He was a good, kind man.

All these belts which went across my breast seemed to me something terrible indeed: I saw that our troubles were not soon to come to an end.

After the giving out of arms, a waggon was brought forward and fifty cartridges a-piece were given out: this augured no good. Then, instead of ordering the ranks to break, and sending us back to our lodgings, Captain Vidal drew his sabre and cried—

"Right file—forward. March!"

The drums beat: I was in despair at not being able at least to thank my hosts for the kindness they had done me; and I said to myself, "They will take me for an ungrateful wretch!" But nevertheless I had to fall in.

We went down a long, crooked street, and suddenly, on the other side the glacis, we found ourselves close to the Rhine, which was covered with ice as far as one could see. On the other side rose lofty mountains, and on their tops old castles, grey and ruinous, like those of the Haut-Bar and the Geroldsech in the Vosges.

The whole battalion crossed the Rhine on the ice. The scene was quite dazzlingly magnificent. We were not alone upon the river. Five or six paces before us, a convoy of powder, guarded by artillerymen, was on its way to Frankfort. The ice was not slippery, but covered with a kind of rugged frost.

When we reached the other side we had to take a

road winding between two ridges. We continued marching thus for five hours, discovering villages to the right and left in the hollow of the hills. Zébédé, who marched beside me, said—

"As we *had* to go, I'm just as well pleased that it's to the war. At least every day we see something new. If we have the luck to return, we can tell all kinds of stories."

"Yes, but I should be better pleased to know less," I said. "I had rather live at my own disposal than at that of others who stay quietly at home while we are climbing here in the snow."

"*You* think nothing about glory," he replied; "glory is something though!"

I answered, "The glory is for others, not for us, Zébédé; for those who are living, eating, sleeping well. They have dances and rejoicings, as we see in the gazettes, and glory into the bargain; while *we* shall have gained it with the sweat of our brows, with fasting and getting our heads broken. Poor devils like us, whom they have forced to start just as it is coming on, lose the habit of labour, and sometimes a limb, and don't get much glory after all. A good many of their old comrades, who were no better than they, who even did not work as hard, have got money during their seven years, have opened shop, married other people's sweethearts, have had fine families, or are men in good repute, municipal councillors, notables. And when those who come back from seeking glory in killing men, pass with their stripes on their arms, they look at them over their shoulders; and if unluckily they have red noses through having drunk brandy to keep their hearts up in the rain and sun and the forced marches, while these others drank good wine, they say, "They're drunkards, these men!" And those conscripts who only asked to remain at home and work, become a kind of beggars. That's what I think, Zébédé: it does not seem to me at all just; I had rather see these friends of glory go and fight themselves, and leave us alone."

"I think as you do," he answered me; "but as we *are* caught, it's better to say that we are fighting for glory. One must always put a good face on things, and make the best of one's position, otherwise, Joseph, we might get laughed at."

Talking of these things and many others, we ended by coming in sight of a great river, which the sergeant told us was the Niem. Near this river was a village on our route; we did not know its name, but we halted there.

We entered the houses, and found brandy, wine, and meat to be sold. Those who had no money ate their crust of brown bread and looked at the others.

About six o'clock in the evening we arrived at Frankfort. This is a city even older than Mayence, and full of Jews. We were taken to a place called Saxenhausen, where we found in barracks the 10th hussars and the Baden *chasseurs*. They told me that this old building had once been a hospital, and I can believe it, for in the interior was a great court with walled arcades; under the arcades horses were lodged, and over them the men.

We arrived at this place across innumerable lanes so narrow that one scarcely saw the stars between the chimney-pots. Captain Florentine and the two lieutenants, Clavel and Bretonville, were waiting for us. After the roll-call, our sergeant led us by detachments to our mess-rooms over the Badeners'. These were large halls with small windows; between the windows were beds.

Sergeant Pinto hung up his canteen on the central

pillar. Each one placed his weapons in the arm-racks, and then disencumbered himself of his knapsack, his blouse and shoes, without saying a word. Zébédé was my bedfellow. Heaven knows we were sleepy. Ten minutes after, we were all sleeping like tops.

CHAPTER X.

It was at Frankfort that I became acquainted with military life. Till then I had been nothing but a mere conscript; now I became a soldier. I am not speaking here of the drill: no! The way to dress to the right or to the left, to lock up, to raise the hand as high as the first or the second ring, to load one's musket, aim, and fire at the word of command—all this is, with a good will to it, the affair of a month or two. But I learned discipline also: to wit; that the corporal always has reason on his side when he speaks to the soldier, the sergeant when he speaks to the corporal, the sergeant-major with the sergeant, the ensign with the sergeant-major, and so on to the marshal of France: even should he say that two and two make five, or that the moon shines at noon-day.

This is rather difficult to get into one's head. But there is a thing which greatly helps one, which is a kind of placard stuck up in the mess-room, and which is read to you from time to time to open your mind. This placard supposes everything that a soldier can have a fancy to do: for instance, to return to his own village, to refuse to serve, to resist his officer, &c., and it always winds up with "Death," or five years of dragging a cannon-ball at least.

The day after our arrival at Frankfort I wrote to M. Goulden, to Catherine, and to Aunt Grédel; one can imagine with what emotion. I related to them my fatigues, the kindness I had received at Mayence, and the courage it had required not to drop behind. I told them also that I continued in good health, thanks to God; that I felt myself stronger than before I left, and that I embraced them a thousand and a thousand times.

I wrote in our mess-room amidst our comrades, and the Phalsbourgians made me add their compliments to their families. Altogether that was a happy moment.

Afterwards I wrote to Mayence to the good people of the *Capougner Strasse*, who had been so helpful to me. I told them how the roll-call had forced me that morning to start off at once, how I had hoped to see them again and thank them, but that the battalion having started for Frankfort, they must needs forgive me.

That very day, in the afternoon, we received our uniforms. Dozens of Jews came quite up to the arcade, and each sold to them his common clothes: I kept only my shirts, shoes, and stockings. The Italians had no end of trouble to make themselves understood by these chapmen, who wished to carry away all for nothing; but the Genoese were as sharp as the Jews, and their disputes were prolonged into the night. Our corporals got well treated by us; it behoved us to make friends of them, seeing that morning and evening they put us through our drill in the courtyard covered with snow. The *cantinière* Christine was always in her corner, her *chaufferette* under her feet. She held in great regard all the young men of family, as she called those who were free with their money. How many let themselves be cozened of their last penny that they might hear themselves called young men of good family! Very soon they were nothing more than beggars! But so it is: vanity, vanity is the ruin of the human race, from conscripts up to generals.

During this time there arrived every day recruits from France, and carts full of the wounded from Poland. What a spectacle before the Hospital of the Holy Ghost, on the other side of the river! It was a procession without an end! All these poor wretches were frost-bitten; some had their noses, some their ears frozen, others an arm, others a leg! They were laid in the snow to prevent them from going to pieces. Never did I see people so miserably clad — with women's petticoats, ragged fur caps, shakos with the crown out, Cossacks' jackets, handkerchiefs and shirts twisted round their feet; they got out of the carts clinging and holding on, and looked at you like wild beasts, their eyes sunk in their heads, their hair bristling up: the gipsies who sleep in nooks in the woods would have had pity on them; and yet these were the best off, because they had escaped from the carnage, while thousands of their comrades had perished in the snow, or on the battle-field.

Klipfel, Zébédé, Fürst and I, went to see these poor wretches; they related to us all the disasters after Moscow, and I perceived then that the terrible twenty-ninth bulletin had only told the truth.

These histories excited us against the Russians; many said—"Ah! if only the war would begin again soon; they'd have a hard job of it this time: it isn't over, it isn't over!" Anger got the better even of me, and sometimes I said to myself—"Why, Joseph, are you losing your head? These Russians are defending their country, their families, and all that men hold most precious in this world. If they had not defended them, one would have a right to despise them."

At this time something very singular occurred.

You must know that Zébédé, my comrade, was the son of the sexton of Phalsbourg, and sometimes amongst ourselves we called him "gravedigger." From us he did not mind it the least. But one evening after drill, as we crossed the court, a hussar cried out,—

"Here, gravedigger! come and help me to drag these trusses of straw."

Zébédé turned round and said,—

"I'm not called gravedigger, and you may just carry your trusses of straw yourself. Do you take me for a brute beast?"

Thereupon the other cried more loudly,—

"Conscript, come, or look to yourself!"

Zébédé, with his great hooked nose, his grey eyes and thin lips, was not blessed with a good temper. He approached the hussar and asked him,—

"What's that you say?"

"I tell you to carry away these trusses of straw, and pretty quickly—do you hear, conscript?"

He was an old fellow with moustache and great red whiskers cut like a hairbrush, *à la mode de Chamboran*. Zébédé clutched him by one of his whiskers; but the other gave him two good blows. Nevertheless a handful of whiskers remained in Zébédé's hand, and as this dispute had attracted a good many lookers-on, the hussar, raising his finger, said,—

"Conscript, you'll hear from me again to morrow-morning."

"All right," said Zébédé, "we shall see. I, too, shall have news for you, old gentleman."

He went straightway to tell me of this, and I, knowing he had never handled anything but a pickaxe, could not help trembling for him.

"Listen, Zébédé," I said, "all that now remains for you to do, since you can't desert, is to go and beg that old fellow's pardon; for all these old ones hit terribly hard: they learnt it in Egypt, Spain and elsewhere. Take my advice! If you will, I'll lend you half-a-crown to stand a bottle of wine with him; that will soften him!"

But he frowned, and would not give in.

"Rather than make excuses," he said, "I should prefer to go and be hanged at once. I scorn all the hussars together. If he has hard hits, I have a long arm, and I have cuts too at my sabre's point, which will pierce his bones as his may my flesh."

Almost immediately the *maître d'armes* Châzy, corporal Fleury, Klipfel, Fürst, Seger, arrived; they all took Zébédé's part, and the *maître d'armes* said that blood must wash out the blow: it was a point of honour with new recruits to fight.

Zébédé replied that the Phalbourgians were not accustomed to be afraid of a blood-letting, and that he was ready. Then the *maître d'armes* went to the captain of the company, named Florentin, the most splendid man that can be imagined—tall, strong, broad-shouldered, straight-nosed, and wearing a decoration bestowed by the Emperor at the banks of the Eylau. The captain thought it quite natural to avenge a blow; he even said it was setting the conscripts a good example, and that if Zébédé did not fight, he would be unworthy to remain in the third battalion of the 6th.

All that night I could not sleep; I heard my comrade snore, and I thought, "Poor Zébédé, to-morrow night you'll be snoring no more!" At last, just as I had fallen asleep towards daybreak, all of a sudden I felt a breath of very cold air; I opened my eyes, and what did

I see but the old red-haired hussar, who had pulled off our bed-coverings, and who said,—

"Come, up sluggard! I'm going to teach you what stuff I'm made of."

"Zébédé rose tranquilly, and replied,—

"I was asleep, veteran: I was asleep."

The other, hearing himself called *veteran,* was about to fall upon my comrade; but two stout fellows who served him for seconds stopped him: and besides, the Phalsbourgians were there as well.

"Come, come, let's make haste!" cried the old soldier.

But Zébédé did not hurry himself in his dressing. Presently he said,—

"Have you permission to go out of quarters, old gentleman?"

"Behind the round-house there is room to deploy."

There was a place overgrown with nettles behind the roundhouse; it was surrounded by a wall, and was easily to be seen from our window, being just below.

Zébédé put on his cloak, and said, turning towards me,—

"Joseph, and you Klipfel, I choose you for my seconds."

But I shook my head.

"Well, then, Fürst; come!" he said.

And all went down together.

I thought all was over with Zébédé: this pained me much, and I thought, "So then, not only the Russians and Prussians exterminate us, but *we* must put our hands to the work too."

The whole mess was at the windows; I alone, at the back, remained seated on my bed. At the end of five minutes, the noise of sabres below turned me quite pale; I seemed not to have a drop of blood in my veins.

But this did not last long, for all at once Klipfel cried out, "A hit!"

Then, I don't know how, I got near a window, and looking over the other's head, I saw the hussar leaning against the wall, and Zébédé raising himself, with his sabre all stained with blood: he had slipt down on his knees during the fight, and the veteran's sabre, which got broken, had only grazed his shoulder, while he, without losing a moment, plunged his own into the hussar's body. If he had not had the good luck to slip, the old man would have pierced his heart.

What I saw was the hussar sinking against the wall, his seconds supporting him under the arms, and Zébédé, pale as death, looking on his sabre, while Klipfel held his cloak to him.

Almost immediately the *reveillé* was sounded, and we went off to the morning roll-call. This was on the 18th of February. The same day we received orders to pack our knapsacks, and we left Frankfort for Selegenstadt, where we remained till the 8th of March. By that time all the recruits had learnt the practice of the musket and platoon-firing. From Selegenstadt we started on the 9th of March for Schweinheim, and on the 24th, 1813, the battalion was re-united with the division at Aschaffenbourg, where we were reviewed by Marshal Ney.

The captain of the company was named Florentin, the lieutenant Bretonville, the commandant of the battalion Gémeau, the adjutant-major Vidal, the colonel of the regiment Zappel, the general of the brigade Ladoncette, and the general of the division Sousham: every soldier ought to know that much, if he does not wish to march like a blind man.

CHAPTER XI.

The snow had begun melting on the 18th or 19th of March. I remember that during the great review of Aschaffenbourg, on a large open space whence one saw the Maine as far as eye could reach, the rain never ceased to fall from ten o'clock in the morning till three o'clock in the afternoon. We had on our left a castle, from the windows of which people looked out quite at their ease, while the water ran into our shoes. On the right the river rushed foaming, discerned dimly as across a mist.

To refresh our ideas, we heard every instant the command "Shoulder arms!"

The marshal advanced slowly, in the midst of his staff. Zébédé was consoled by thinking that we were about to see the "*bravest of the brave.*" For my part, I thought "If I could see all this by the fireside, it would please me more."

At last he appeared before us; and I see him still,

with his great hat soaked with rain, his coat covered with embroidery and decorations, and his great boots. He was a fine-looking man, with reddish blonde hair and complexion, high nose and terribly strong-looking. He was not proud, for, as he passed before the company, and the captain presented arms, all of a sudden he turned round on his great horse, and said out loud,—

"Why, that's Florentin!"

The captain drew himself up without knowing what to say. It seems that the marshal and he had been in the ranks together at the time of the Republic. The captain said at last,—

"Yes, Marshal, 'tis Sebastian Florentin."

"Faith, Florentin," said the marshal, stretching out his arm in the direction of Russia, "I'm glad to see you again; I thought you had been left lying there."

All our company were pleased, and Zébédé said to me,—

"That's what I call a man: I would get knocked on the head for him."

I couldn't see why Zébédé should want to be knocked on the head because the marshal had said "How do you do?" to an old comrade.

That's all I remember of Aschaffenbourg.

In the evening we went in again to eat our soup at Schweinheim, a place rich in wines, hemp, and corn, where almost everybody looked at us with unfriendly eyes.

We lodged by threes or fours in the houses, like so many bailiff's men, and had meat every day, either beef, mutton, or bacon. The household bread was very good, and the wine too; but several of us affected to find everything bad, thinking thereby to pass for great lords: they were much mistaken, for I heard the towns-people say in German,—

"Those fellows in their own country are beggars! If one went to France to look, one would not even find potatoes in their cellars."

And they were not mistaken.

For my part, I was very well content to be cossetted in this fashion, and I should have liked it to last through the whole campaign. Two conscripts from St.-Dié were with me at the village-postmaster's: his horses had almost all been put in requisition for our cavalry. This could not have put him into a good humour; but he said nothing, and smoked his pipe behind the stove from morning till night. His wife was a tall strong woman, and his two daughters were very pretty; they were afraid of us, and ran away when we returned from drill, or from mounting guard at the end of the village.

The evening of the fourth day, as we were finishing our supper, there came in about seven o'clock an old man with white hair, and of a most respectable appearance. He saluted us, and said in German to the postmaster,—

"These are new recruits?"

"Yes, M. Steuger," answered the other, "we shall never get rid of those fellows. If I could poison them all, it would be soon done."

I turned quietly round and said,—

"I know German; don't say such things."

Scarcely had the postmaster heard me speak, than his long pipe almost fell from his hand.

"You are very rash in your words, M. Kalkreuch," said the old man; "if any besides this young man had heard you, think of what would happen to you."

"It's only a way of talking," replied the big man. "Why, what can you expect when everything is taken from you? when you are being ruined for years? One loses one's head at last, and one speaks at random."

The old man, who was no other than the pastor of Schweinheim, then came to salute me and said,—

"Sir, your way of acting is that of a gentleman; believe me, M. Kalkreuch is incapable of doing harm even to an enemy."

"I think so, too, sir," I answered, "otherwise I should not be eating his sausages with such a relish."

The postmaster, hearing these words, began to laugh like a child, laying his two big hands on his stomach, and saying, "I could never have believed that a Frenchman could make me laugh."

My two comrades being on guard, they went out, and I remained alone. Then the postmaster went to fetch a bottle of old wine; he sat down to the table and wished me to drink with him, which I did willingly. From that time till our departure these persons had great confidence in me. Every evening we talked by the fireside; the pastor came, and the young girls themselves came down to listen. They were *blondes* with blue eyes; one might have been eighteen years old, the other twenty: I found in them a likeness to Catherine, which touched my heart.

It was known that I had a sweetheart in my own

country, because I had not been able to keep from saying so, and that affected them.

The postmaster complained bitterly of the French; the pastor said that they were a vain and profligate nation, and that on this account all Germany was rising up against us; that they were weary of the vices of our soldiers and the rapacity of our generals, and that the Rugend band* had been formed to resist us.

"At first," he said, "you spoke to us of liberty; we loved to hear of it, and our wishes were rather for your armies than for those of the King of Prussia and the Emperor of Austria: you made war on our soldiers and not on us; you maintained ideas that every one felt to be just and grand, and that is why you have not had to fight the people, but their masters. *Now* it is very different; all Germany is ready to march, all the young men are rising, and it is we who shall speak of liberty, of virtue and of justice, to France. Whoever speaks of these things is always the strongest, because he has against him only the rascals of all countries, and with him youth and courage and great ideas: all that raises the soul above egotism, and makes you sacrifice your life without regret. You had that for

* "League of Virtue."

a long time, but you have got tired of it. Your generals, once I remember, fought for liberty; they slept on straw in barns, like common soldiers: they were terrible men! Now they must have sofas; they are nobler than our nobles, richer than our bankers. Thus it is that war, formerly so noble a thing—an art, a sacrifice, a devotion to our country—has become a trade, which answers better than keeping a shop. It's always a very fine thing, because you wear epaulettes; but still there's a difference between fighting for eternal ideas and fighting for the good of your shop.

"Now-a-days it is *our* turn to speak of liberty and one's country; and that is why I think this war will be fatal to you. Every man capable of thought, from the simple student to the professor of theology, is about to march against you. You have at your head the greatest general in the world; but we have eternal justice. You think you have on your side the Saxons, Bavarians, Badeners, and the Hessians; undeceive yourselves: the children of old Germany know well that the greatest of crimes and the greatest of shames is to fight against our brothers. Let the kings make allowances—the people will be against you in spite of these allowances: they will defend their blood, their country, which God forces us to love, and which one cannot betray without crime. All will fall upon you: the Austrians will massacre you if they can, in spite of the marriage of Marie Louise and your Emperor. People begin to see that the interests of kings are not everything in this world, and the greatest genius cannot change the nature of things."

Thus spoke the pastor very seriously. I did not then very well understand his talk, and I said to myself, "Words are words and musket-shots are musket-shots. If we encounter only students and professors of theology on the battlefield, all will go well. As to the rest, discipline will always prevent the Hessians, Bavarians, and Saxons from turning; just as it obliges us to fight, though more than one has no desire for it. Does not the soldier obey the corporal, the corporal the sergeant, and so on up to the marshal, who does what the king pleases? It's plain that the pastor has never served in a regiment, or he would know that these ideas are nothing, and that the orders are everything; but I don't care to contradict him, for the postmaster wouldn't bring me any more a bottle of wine after supper. Let them think what they please, all that I desire is to encounter none but theologians."

Whilst we were talking thus, all at once, on the morning of the 27th of March, came marching orders. The battalion halted the first night at Lauterbach, next day at New Kirchen: we did nothing but march, march. Those who were not already accustomed to carrying a knapsack, could not complain of want of exercise: for Heaven be praised! we made considerable way. For me, I had long left off sweating under my cartridge-box with fifty cartridges, my knapsack, and my musket on my shoulder; nor do I know that I limped any longer.

We were not the only troops in movement; everything was on the march: everywhere one met regiments on their way—detachments of cavalry, trains of artillery, convoys of powder and shot; and all were moving on towards Erfurt, as after a deluge of rain numberless streams find their way everywhere to the river.

Our sergeants said to each other, "We are coming near: we shall have hot work!" And we thought, "So much the better! These rascally Russians and Prussians are the cause of our being taken; if they had remained quiet, we should have been still in France!"

This idea gave us a great feeling of bitterness.

Besides one finds everywhere people who like nothing so well as fighting. Klipfel and Zébédé spoke of falling upon the Prussians, and I, that I might not seem less courageous than the others, also said how rejoiced I was.

On the 8th of April, the battalion entered the citadel of Erfurt, a very strong and very rich place. I shall always remember that at the moment when we broke up our ranks on the *Place* before the barracks, the officer in charge of the baggage handed a packet of letters to the sergeant of the company. Among the number was one for me: I recognised at once Catherine's handwriting, which produced on me such an effect that my knees trembled!

Zébédé took my musket, saying, "Come then!" He too was very glad to hear news of Phalsbourg.

I had hidden my letter deep in my pocket, and all those of my country followed me to hear it read. But I wanted to be seated on my bed in quiet before opening it; and only when we were in barracks in a corner of Tinchmatt, and my musket in the gun-rack, did I begin. All the others bent over my shoulder. Tears flowed down my cheeks, because Catherine told me how she prayed for me. My comrades hearing that, said—

"We are sure that we are prayed for, too!" One spoke of his mother, another of his sisters, another of his sweetheart.

At the end, M. Goulden had written that all the town was well, that I must take courage, that these miseries were but for a time. He charged me above all to let my comrades know that they were remembered, and that their parents grieved at not receiving a single word of news about them.

This letter was a great comfort to us all; and when I reflected that this was the 8th of April, and that the battles were soon going to begin, I regarded it as our country's last farewell to half of us. Many were never to hear again of their parents, their friends, and those who loved them in this world.

CHAPTER XII.

All this, as Sergeant Pinto said, was only the opening of the ball: the dancing was scarcely begun.

Meanwhile we did duty at the citadel with a battalion of the 27th, and from the top of the ramparts we saw all the environs covered with troops, some bivouacking, others quartered in the villages.

On the 18th, returning from mounting guard at the door of Warthan, the sergeant, who had taken a friendship for me, said,—

"Fusilier Bertha, the Emperor has come."

Nobody had yet heard this mentioned, and I answered—

"Begging your pardon, sergeant, I have just been having a glass with the sapper Merlin at the general's door, and he told me nothing about that."

He gave me a wink and said,—

"All the world's up and stirring. You don't yet understand that, conscript. But he is there—I feel it to the soles of my feet. When he is not come, everything limps, as it were; and now, see down there! look at those expresses galloping along the roads: everything is reviving. Wait for the first dance; wait, and you will see. The Kaiserliks and the Cossacks have no need of their spectacles to see if he is with us: they feel it at once."

So saying, the sergeant laughed in his long moustaches.

I had a presentiment that great misfortunes might be coming upon me, yet I was forced to put a good face upon it.

In fact the sergeant was not mistaken, for that same day about three o'clock in the afternoon, all the troops quartered around the town were in movement, and at five o'clock we were ordered to be in arms. The Marshal Prince de la Moskowa entered the town in the midst of a great number of officers and generals who composed his staff. Almost immediately General Souham, a grey old general, entered the citadel, and reviewed us on the *Place*. He said in a loud voice, so that all the world could hear—

"Soldiers! you are about to form part of the vanguard of the 3rd corps: remember that you are Frenchmen. *Vive l'Empereur!*"

Then everybody shouted "*Vive l'Empereur!*" which produced a terrific effect in the echoes of the *Place*, and the general went away again with Colonel Yappel.

That same night we were relieved by the Hessians, and we quitted Erfurt with the 10th hussars and a regiment of Baden *chasseurs*. At six or seven o'clock in the morning we were before the city of Weimar; we saw in the light of the rising sun its gardens, churches, and houses, with an old castle on the right.

We were made to bivouack here, and the hussars went out as scouts into the town. Towards nine o'clock, whilst we were cooking our soup, we heard, all of a sudden, far off, the crack of musket-shots. Our hussars had fallen in with Prussian hussars in the streets, had fought and exchanged pistol-shots with them. But it was too far off for us to see the combat.

At the end of an hour the hussars returned: they had lost two men. It was thus that the campaign began.

We remained at Weimar five days, during which the whole of the 3rd corps came up. As we were the vanguard, we had to march again in the direction of the Sulza and of Warthan. It was then we first saw the enemy—Cossacks, who always retreated out of reach of our fire; so the more they retreated, the more courageous we became.

What annoyed me was to hear Zébédé say in an ill-humoured manner,—

"Will they never come to a halt, then?"

I thought, "If they go away, what better can we wish for? We shall have won without getting any harm."

But at last they halted on the other side of a large and deep river; and we saw a number of them waiting to cut us to pieces, if we had the ill-luck to cross this river.

It was on the 29th of April, when the dusk was coming on; one could not see a finer sunset. On the other side of the water, a plain stretched as far as the eye could see, and on the red strip of the horizon swarmed these horsemen, with shakos turned up in front, green jackets, a cartridge pouch under the arm, and sky-blue trousers: there were also numbers of Lancers behind. Sergeant Pinto recognized them as mounted Russian *chasseurs* and Cossacks. He recognized the river too, and said that it was the Saale.

We came as close as we could to the river edge to fire at these horsemen, who retreated further and disappeared quite into the red horizon. We then made our bivouac beside the river, sentinels being placed. We had a large village behind us on our left, and a detachment went there to try to get meat by paying for it; for since the Emperor's arrival, there had been orders to pay for everything.

In the night, while we were cooking, other regiments of the division arrived. They too bivouacked along the shore, and it was something magnificent to see these long lines of fire quivering on the water.

Nobody cared to sleep. Zébédé, Klipfel, Fürst, and I were messing together, and we said to each other,—

"To-morrow there'll be hot work, if we mean to cross the river. Our Phalsbourg friends, who are taking their pint at the brewery of the *Homme Sauvage* have no idea that we are seated in this place, on a river's side, eating a piece of veal, and that we are going to sleep on the ground, and lay up the rheumatism for our old age; not to speak of gun-shots and sabre strokes which are in store for us, perhaps sooner than we think."

"Bah!" said Klipfel, "this is life. I don't care to sleep in cotton and pass one day just like another. If one would live, one must be well off one day, ill off the next: variety is charming. As for gunshots, sabre and bayonet-thrusts, Heaven be praised, we can give as many as we take!"

"Yes," said Zébédé, lighting his pipe, "for my part, I hope that if I chance to lose an arm, it will not be for not having paid back the blows I have got."

We had been talking thus for two or three hours, when the sentinel called out—

"Who goes there?"

"France!"

"What regiment?"

"Sixth of the line!"

It was Marshal Ney with General Brenier, followed by pontoon-officers and guns. The Marshal had answered "Sixth of the line," because he knew beforehand where we were; this delighted us, and even made us prouder. We saw him pass on horseback with General Souham, and five or six other general officers, and notwithstanding the night we recognised them perfectly: the sky was glittering with stars, the moon was rising, and it was almost as light as in broad day.

They stopped at a winding of the river, where six guns were stationed, and almost immediately after the pontoon-men came up with a long file of carriages loaded with pontoons, planks, and all that was needed for throwing two bridges across. Our hussars galloped along the riverside to collect the boats, and the gunners were at their pieces ready to sweep away those who might try to hinder the work. For a long while we watched the progress of the works; from time to time were heard shouts of "Who goes there?" It was the regiments of the third corps coming in.

About daybreak I fell asleep; Klipfel had to shake me to wake me up. The roll-call was being beaten on all sides; the bridges were finished, and we were to cross the Saale.

A heavy dew was falling; every one hastened to dry his piece, roll up his cloak, and buckle it on his knapsack. We helped each other and fell into rank. It was about four o'clock in the morning. A fog rising from the river made all look grey. Already two battalions had passed over the bridges, the men in file, the officers and the colours in the midst; a dull rumbling sound followed, and then the guns and the waggons crossed.

Captain Florentin had just made us look to our priming, when Generals Souham and Chemineau, Colonel Zappel and our commandant arrived. The battalion began to march. I was always looking to see if the Russians were not galloping up; but nothing stirred.

By degrees, as we reached the other side, every regiment formed squares, with their muskets grounded. About five o'clock the whole division had passed. The sun had dispersed the mist, and we saw about three quarters of a league on our right an old city with pointed roofs, a cupola-formed bell-tower covered with slate with a cross on the top, and further on a castle; this was Weissenfels.

Between the town and us lay a deep hollow. Marshal Ney, who also had just come up, wished first of all to know what might be within it. Two companies of the twenty-seventh were deployed as skirmishers. The squares moved forward at the usual pace; the officers, sappers, and drummers in the centre, the guns in the space between, the waggons bringing up the rear.

Everybody mistrusted this hollow; all the more because we had seen, the day before, a large body of cavalry which could not have retired to the end of the great plain, the whole extent of which lay open to us: it was impossible. Never did I feel a greater misgiving: I expected something. In spite of that, the sight of us all thus drawn up, with muskets loaded, colours in front, our generals behind, and all full of confidence—we marching on without hurry, the whole mass stepping in time; all this filled us with courage. I said to myself,—"Perhaps at the sight of us they will fly: that will be decidedly the best for them and for us."

I was in the second rank, behind Zébédé in front, and it may be supposed that I kept my eyes open. From time to time I glanced sideways at the other square, which was advancing on the same line, and I saw the Marshal in the centre, with his staff: they raised their heads, with their large hats on one side, to see what was passing at a distance.

The skirmishers now drew near the ravine bordered with brushwood and quick-set hedges. Already, some minutes before, I had perceived further off on the other side something moving and glistening, like ears of corn when the wind passes, and the idea occurred to me that the Russians with their lances and their sabres might be there; I had, however, a difficulty in believing it. But at the moment that our skirmishers approached the enemy's force, and the firing began in several places, I saw clearly that they *were* lances. Almost immediately a flash, as of lightning, came right in our faces, and the cannon roared. These Russians had guns; they had just fired at us, and, some noise having made me turn my head, I saw that there was a gap in our ranks, to the left.

At the same time I heard Colonel Zapfel quietly give the order—

"Close up your ranks!"

And Captain Florentin repeated it.

This was done so quickly that I had no time for reflection. But fifty paces further off there was another flash and a like noise in the ranks, like a strong wind passing, and I saw another hole, this time to the right.

And as, after each volley from the Russians, the colonel always said,—"Close up." I understood that each time there was a gap! I dared not think of it, and tried to turn my thoughts away; when General Chemineau, who had just entered our square, cried in a terrific voice,—

"Halt!"

I looked, and saw that the Russians were coming on in full force.

"First rank, kneel; fix bayonets!" cried the general. "Shoulder arms!"

As Zébédé had knelt down, I was in a manner in

the first rank. I still seem to see advancing all that mass of horses and of Russians bending forward sabre in hand, and to hear our general say, quietly behind us, as at drill,—

"Ready—present—fire!"

We had fired, the four squares together: it seemed as if the sky was going to fall. Scarcely had the smoke cleared off a little, than we saw the Russians flying back again at full gallop; but our guns thundered, and our bullets went faster than their horses.

"Charge!" cried the general.

I think I never in my life felt such pleasure.

"There! they're going off!" I said to myself. And from all sides we heard the cry, "Vive l'Empereur!"

In my joy, I set to shouting like the rest. This lasted a full minute. The squares were formed in marching order again: we thought that all was over; but at two or three hundred paces from the ravine, a great noise was heard, and for the second time the general cried,—

"Halt! Kneel! Fix bayonets!"

The Russians swept out of the hollow like the wind to fall upon us: they came on altogether. We heard no more orders; but the natural good sense of French soldiers suggested to them to fire on the mass, and the file-firing began to roll like the rattling of the drums at a great review: those who have not heard the sound, can form no idea of it. Some of the Russians came right up to us; we saw them through the smoke, then immediately after, one could see no more.

After a few minutes, while we still did nothing but load and fire, the terrible voice of General Chemineau shouted, "Cease firing!"

One could scarcely dare obey; each one hastened to discharge one more shot; but, the smoke being dispersed, we saw this great mass of cavalry going up the other side of the ravine.

The squares were deployed in order to march in column. The drums beat to the charge, our cannon thundered. "Forward! forward! Vive l'Empereur!"

We descended into the ravine, over the heaps of horses and Russians still stirring upon the ground, and we then re-ascended at double-quick time in the direction of Weissenfels. All these Cossacks and chasseurs were galloping before us as fast as they could: the battle was won!

But, at the moment when we approached the city gardens, their guns, which they had brought with them, came to a stand behind a kind of orchard, and sent us some balls, one of which broke the hatchet of the sapper Merlin and knocked off his head. The corporal of the sappers, Thomé, also had his arm fractured by a piece of the hatchet; and it was necessary to amputate it that evening at Weissenfels. It was then that we began to run; for the quicker one moves, the less time have the others to fire: every one understood that.

We entered the town by three places, crossing hedges and gardens; passing between hop-poles, and leaping over walls. The marshal and generals rushed after us. Our regiment entered by an avenue bordered with poplars, which skirted the cemetery, and as we debouched on the Place, another column arrived by the main street.

There we halted, and the marshal, without losing a minute, detached the 27th to go and seize a bridge, and try to cut off the enemy's retreat. During this time the rest of the division arrived, and was drawn up in order on the Place. The burgomaster and the councillors of Weissenfels were already at the gate of the Hotel de Ville to welcome us.

When we had all re-formed, the Marshal Prince de la Moskowa passed before our front, and said to us, joyously,—

"Very well! very well! I am content with you! The Emperor will know of your excellent conduct. You have done well!"

He could not keep from laughing, because we had run so close upon the guns.

General Souham said to him, "Things go on well;" and he replied, "Yes, yes: 'tis in the blood, 'tis in the blood."

As for me, I rejoiced to have come so well out of the business.

The battalion remained there till the next day. We were lodged among the townspeople, who were afraid of us, and who gave us all we asked for. The 27th came in again in the evening, and was lodged in the old castle. We were very tired. After having smoked two or three pipes together, talking about our glory, Zébédé, Klipfel, and I went to sleep in the shop of a joiner on a heap of shavings, and we remained there till midnight, the moment at which the roll-call was sounded. We were then obliged to get up; the joiner gave us brandy, and we went out. Rain was falling in torrents. That same night the battalion went to bivouack before the village of Clepen, two hours off from Weissenfels; not at all too happy, on account of the rain.

Several other detachments came to join us. The Emperor had arrived at Weissenfels; the whole of the third corps had to follow us. Nothing was talked of but this the whole day; many rejoiced at it. But on the morrow, towards five o'clock in the morning, the battalion marched away.

In front of us flowed a river called the Rippach. Instead of turning aside to gain a bridge, we crossed it on the spot. The water came up to our waists, and I thought, as I pulled my shoes out of the mud, "If any one had told me this in the days when I was afraid of catching a cold in the head at M. Goulden's, and when I changed my stockings twice a week, I should never have believed it. Well, strange things happen to one in this life."

As we went along the river's bank on the other side among the rushes, we discovered on the heights to the left a band of Cossacks who were watching us.

They followed us slowly without daring to attack, and then I saw that after all mud was good for something.

We had been going on thus for more than an hour; it was now broad day, when all at once a terrible firing and the rumbling of cannon made us turn our heads in the direction of Clepen. The commandant, on horseback, was looking over the reeds.

This lasted a long time. Sergeant Pinto said, "The division is advancing; it is attacked."

The Cossacks looked also, and did not disappear till an hour after. Then we saw the division advance in column to the right, along the plain, chasing masses of Russian cavalry.

"Forward!" cried the commandant. And we ran without knowing why, still going down the river, till we reached an old bridge where the Rippach and the Gorma unite. We meant to stop the enemy at this spot, but the Cossacks had already discovered our scheme, and their whole army retired across the Gorma, passing by a ford. The division having rejoined us, we learned that Marshal Bessières had just been killed by a cannon-ball.

We marched from this bridge to go and bivouack before the village of Gorschen. The rumour ran that a great battle was imminent, and that all that had passed till then was but a mere beginning, to try if the recruits could stand fire. After that, any one may imagine the reflections made by a man of sense who was there against his will, amongst such reckless beings as Fürst,

Zébédé, and Klipfel, who were rejoicing as if such event could bring *them* anything but musket, sabre, or bayonet wounds.

All the rest of that day and even part of the night, thinking of Catherine, I prayed God to guard my life, and that I might keep my hands, which are necessary to the poor for the earning of their livelihood.

CHAPTER XIII.

Fires were lighted on the hill in front of Gross Gorschen, and a detachment descended to the village and brought us back five or six old cows to boil down for soup; but we were so fatigued that many were more fain to sleep than to eat. Other regiments arrived with cannon and ammunition, and towards eleven o'clock we were in number there ten or twelve thousand men, and in the village two thousand, the whole of Souham's division. The general and his orderlies were lodged in a great mill to the left, near a stream called the Floss Graben.

I too at last fell asleep, worn out with fatigue; but I woke up every hour of the night. We heard behind us a continual noise in the direction of the road from the old bridge of Poserna, which extends to Lutzen and Leipzig: the roll of carriages, cannon, and waggons kept rising and falling in the silence.

Sergeant Pinto did not sleep; he smoked his pipe while drying his feet at the fire. Whenever one or another moved he wanted to talk.

"Well! conscript," he said,—

But we made as though we did not hear him, turned round yawning and fell asleep again.

The clock of Gross Gorschen struck six when I awoke; my thighs and loins seemed broken with such long marching in the mire. The fires smouldered, only ashes and a few embers remained. The sergeant stood looking on the white plain, on which the sun was shedding some streaks of gold.

All the troops slept around us, with their feet to the fires; some snored, or talked in their dreams.

The sergeant, seeing me awake, took an ember for his pipe, and said,—

"Well, Fusilier Bertha, we are the rear-guard now."

I did not very well understand him.

"You are surprised, conscript," he said; "it's clear enough though: *we* haven't stirred, but the army has gone right about; yesterday it was there before us on the Rippach, now it's behind us, near Lutzen; instead of being at the head we are at the tail."

"And what do we get by it?" I asked.

"Why, we get this—that we shall be the first to reach Leipzig and fall upon the Prussians. You'll understand it presently, conscript."

Then I raised myself to look at the country, and I saw before me an extensive swampy plain, traversed by the Gonna-Bach and the Floss Graben; some small hills rose beside these streams, and in the background flowed a large river, which the sergeant told me was the Elster. The morning mists were spread over the whole.

I turned and discerned behind us, in the valley, the steeple of Gross Gorschen, and further off, right and left, five or six little hamlets, built in the hollows of the hills; for it is a country of hills, and Kaya, Eisdorf, Starsiedel, Rahna, Klein Gorschen, and Gross Gorschen, are between them, beside little lakes, where grow poplars, willows, and aspens. The third division occupied the villages, the head-quarters being at Kaya.

At seven o'clock the "reveillé" was sounded; we went down into the village to fetch wood, straw, or hay; carriages arrived, and bread and cartouches were distributed. We were to remain there, to let the army defile upon Leipzig; which was why Sergeant Pinto said that we should be the rear-guard.

Two cantinières also came from the village, and as I had still five six-franc-pieces, I offered a glass to Klipfel and Zébédé, to keep off the damp of the night. I ventured to offer one to Sergeant Pinto too, who accepted it, saying, "that brandy with one's bread warms one's heart."

In short, we were quite happy, and no one suspected the terrible things which were to happen that day. We thought the Russians were looking for us far off behind the Gruna-Bach; but they knew where we were. Suddenly, at ten o'clock, General Souham, in the midst of his officers, ascended the ridge at full gallop: he had just learnt something. I was just then standing sentry near the stacks of arms; I seem still to see him, with his grey hair and large hat with a white border, advancing to the edge of the hill, fixing a long glass and looking; then turning quickly back, and descending to the village with the command to beat to arms.

All the sentinels fell back, and Zébédé, who had the eyes of a hawk, said,—

"I see there, below the Elster, masses swarming; there are some advancing in regular order, and others coming from the marshes across three bridges. What a deluge, if they should all fall upon us!"

"Aye," said Sergeant Pinto, his nose in the air, and his hand screening his eyes, "'tis the beginning of a battle, or *I* know nothing about it. While our army is defiling on Leipzig, and extending to more than three leagues, these rascally Russians and Prussians are trying to take us in flank with their whole force and cut us in two. It's well devised on their part: they learn something of the tricks of war every day!"

"But what are *we* to do?" asked Klipfel.

"Why, that's simple enough," answered the sergeant; "we are here some 12,000 or 15,000 men, who have never retreated an inch; we shall stick like nails, one to six or seven, till the Emperor shall be informed of the affair and fall back to help us. Look, there are the orderlies setting off already."

It was true: five or six officers crossed the plain of Lutzen behind us on the Leipzig side; they came like the wind. I prayed God in my heart to allow the army to come in time to succour us; for to know that one must perish is a terrible thing.

Sergeant Pinto went on,—

"You are in luck, conscripts; if one or another of you escapes, he may boast of having seen a very pretty thing. Just see those blue lines advancing, shouldering their muskets, along the Floss Graben; each of those lines is a regiment: there are thirty of them, that makes 60,000 Prussians, without counting the masses of horse, which are so many squadrons. And to the left of them near the Rippach, those others who advance shining in the sun, are the dragoons and cuirassiers of the Russian imperial guard; I saw them for the first time at Austerlitz, where we gave them a proper dressing: there are full 18,000 or 20,000. Those masses of spears behind are bands of Cossacks; so in an hour we shall enjoy the advantage of looking in the whites of the eyes of 100,000 men, the most stubborn fellows in all Russia and Prussia. To speak truth, 'twill be a battle in which to gain the cross; and if one does *not* gain it, one must never hope to do so."

"You think so, sergeant?" said Zébédé, who never had two clear ideas in his head, and who fancied himself already in possession of the cross. His eyes glittered like those of a sanguine simpleton as he was.

"Aye," replied the sergeant, "for we are going to close up: and suppose in the mêlée one sees a colonel, a gun, a standard, something that strikes the eye! you spring upon it, across bayonets, sabres, rammers, what not; one seizes it, and if one comes out again one is recommended."

Whilst he said this I thought how the Mayor of Felsenbourg had received the cross for having led out his village folk in carriages adorned with garlands to meet Marie Louise, singing old *lieds* (songs), and I thought *his* manner of winning the cross much more convenient than that of Sergeant Pinto.

I had no time to think more about it, for on all sides the drums were beating to arms; each ran to the place where the weapons of his company were stacked, and hastened to seize his musket. The officers set us in battle order, cannon arrived at full gallop from the village: they were placed at the top of the hill, a little at the back, that the ridge might serve to cover them. All was agitation in the other villages as well; but we were the first on whom the mass would fall.

The enemy had halted at twice the distance of cannon-range, and their cavalry hovered in hundreds round us to reconnoitre. Only to look at these hosts of Prussians blackening both sides of the river, and the foremost lines beginning to form in column, made me say to myself,—"This time, Joseph, all is lost: all is over!—there's no help for it! All you can do is to revenge yourself,—defend yourself, and have pity on none."

"Form square!" was now the cry; and we formed four squares of four battalions each. This time I was quite inside, which gave me pleasure; for I thought that the Prussians, advancing in three columns, would naturally first attack the front. But scarcely had I entertained the idea, than a perfect hail of bullets swept the square. The noise of cannon thundered, too, from a hill on the left: there were there thirty pieces; it may be imagined what gaps they made in our ranks.

The cannon-balls whistled sometimes in the air, sometimes in the ranks, and sometimes they entered the ground, which they tore up with a fearful noise.

Our cannon also volleyed in a manner to prevent one from hearing the half of the whistling and roaring of the other; but it availed nothing: and, besides, what produced the worst effect was, the officers incessantly repeating, "Close up the ranks!"

We were in a dense smoke, without having yet fired, and I said to myself, "If we stay here a quarter of an hour, we shall be massacred without being able to defend ourselves;" which seemed to me terribly hard. Then all of a sudden the columns of the Prussians came up between the two hills, making a strange noise like the rising of an inundation. Immediately the three foremost sides of our square, slanting right and left, fired. Heaven knows how many Prussians remained in this hollow! But instead of stopping, their comrades continued to ascend, yelling like wolves, "Vaterland! Vaterland!" all their battalion firing at a hundred paces off into our bodies.

After that began thrusts with the bayonet, and blows dealt with the butt-ends of their muskets; they were so furiously bent on breaking us. All my life I shall remember how a battalion of these Prussians came up at our side, dealing us thrusts with the bayonet which we repaid without quitting our ranks, and that they were all mown down by two pieces which happened to be in position behind the square.

No other troops were now willing to attack our squares. The enemy went down the hill again, and we had loaded our guns to exterminate them to a man. Then their guns again opened fire, and we heard a loud noise to our right; it was their cavalry coming to avail themselves of the gaps made by their cannon. I saw nothing of this attack, for it took place on the other side of the division; but meanwhile the balls swept us away by dozens: General Chemineau had his thigh broken. The affair evidently could not go on much longer, and we were ordered to retreat; which we did with a pleasure easy to understand.

We passed round Gross Gorschen, followed by the Prussians, with whom we exchanged a running fire. The 2,000 men who were in the village checked the enemy by a rolling fire from all the windows, during which we reascended the ridge to gain the second village, Klein Gorschen. But then all the Prussian cavalry came upon our flank to cut off our retreat, and force us to remain under the fire of their pieces. This aroused in me an inconceivable indignation. I heard Zébédé call out,—
"Let us rush on them, rather than stay here!"

It was indeed fearfully dangerous, for these regiments of hussars and chasseurs advanced in good order before finally rushing to the charge. We kept on retreating, when from the top of the ridge came the order, "Halt!" and in the same moment the hussars, who were already rushing upon us, received a terrible volley of grapeshot which knocked them over by hundreds. It was from the division Girard, which had formed a battery of six pieces, a little to the right. This produced a very good effect; the hussars retired faster than they had come, and the six squares of the division Girard were united to ours at Klein Gorschen, to check the Prussian infantry, who kept on advancing, the three first columns in front, and three others as strong behind.

We had lost Gross-Gorschen; but now, between Klein-Gorschen and Rahna, the affair soon became more terrible still.

I now thought of nothing but revenging myself. I had become, one may say, mad with anger against those who wished to take my life—the possession of every man, which each one ought to guard as well as he can. I felt a sort of hatred for these Prussians, whose cries and insolent looks revolted my heart. I had great pleasure in seeing Zébédé still near me, and as while waiting for a new attack our arms lay at our feet, I grasped his hand.

"We have been in luck!" he said. "But may the Emperor only come up soon, for they are twenty times more than we: may he but come with cannon!"

He talked no more about getting the cross!

I looked a little aside to see if the sergeant was still there, and I saw him quietly cleaning his bayonet: his face was unchanged; which rejoiced me. I would have been glad to know if Klipfel and Fürst were still in their ranks; but the command "Shoulder arms!" made me think of something else.

The three first hostile columns had halted on the hill of Gross-Gorschen to await the three others, who advanced musket on shoulder. The village between us in the valley was on fire, the thatched roofs blazed, the smoke rose to heaven, and on the left hand we saw coming across the ploughed field, a long file of cannon to take us on the flank.

About midday the six columns were in march, and large bodies of hussars and mounted chasseurs were deployed on both sides of Gross-Gorschen. The cannon pealed from either side; our drums beating sounded but like the buzzing of a fly in a storm, and at the bottom of the valley, the Prussians shouted all together, "Vaterland! Vaterland!"

As they climbed the height, their battalion-fire covered us with smoke; we responded with file-firing; nothing more was seen or heard for a quarter of an hour, when all of a sudden the Prussian hussars were in our square. I know not how it happened, but there they were, galloping right and left, and leaning down from their small horses to cut us down without mercy. We gave them bayonet-thrusts, we shouted, they discharged their pistols at us; in short, it was terrible. Zébédé, Sergeant Pinto, and some twenty more of us, kept together. I shall behold all my life those pale faces, their moustaches extending behind their ears, their little shakos fastened tight under their jaws. I shall never cease to hear the cries raised in German and in French: they called us "*Schweinpelz!*" and old Sergeant Pinto never stopped crying, "Courage, boys! courage!"

How we got out of this I know not; we marched at random amidst the smoke, the firing, and the sabre-cuts. All that I remember is that Zébédé cried to me every moment, "Come on, come on!" and that at last seven or eight of us were in a sloping field behind a square which still held its ground. I looked and saw that my bayonet had blood and hair at the point, which shows that in my fury I had dealt frightful blows.

At the end of a minute old Pinto said, "The regiment is routed. Those rascally Prussians have sabred half of them. We shall fall in with it again presently; for the present we have to hinder the enemy from entering the village.

We descended a short flight of steps which led into a garden in Klein-Gorschen, and we entered a house, the door of which that opened from the fields the sergeant barricaded with a great kitchen-table; then showing us the street-door, he said,—

"There is our retreat."

After that, we ascended to the first story and entered a good-sized room, which had two windows looking on the village and two on the smoke-covered hill where the file-firing continued to blaze and the cannon to roll. In an alcove there was a bed that had been slept in, and beside the bed a cradle: the people had no doubt fled before the battle began; but a dog, with a great white tail, pricked up ears, and sharp nose half hidden in the curtains, looked at us with glittering eyes. All this seems to return on me like a dream.

The sergeant opened the window and fired into the street, where two or three Prussian hussars were advancing; the rest stood behind him on their guard. I looked another way, to see if the square still held their ground, and I saw them five or six hundred paces off, retreating in good order, and firing from all the four sides on the mass of cavalry who surrounded them. Across the ranks I saw the colonel, a short stout man on horseback in the centre, and close to him the colours, so torn that nothing was left but a rag hanging all down the staff.

Further on, to the left, a hostile column debouched

at the turn of the road, and marched on Klein-Gorschen. This column endeavoured to cut off our retreat into the village; but hundreds of disbanded soldiers had come up before us, and were still coming in from all sides, some turning at every fifty paces to fire a shot, others wounded, and dragging themselves on towards a resting-place. They entered the houses, and as the column continued approaching, a rolling fire greeted it from all the windows. This checked it; all the more that at the same instant, on the ridge to the right, the divisions Brenier and Marchand began to deploy, having been sent by the Prince de la Moskowa to our assistance. We heard afterwards that Marshal Ney had followed the Emperor in the direction of Leipzig, and returned at hearing the roll of cannon.

The Prussians halted then in this place, and the firing ceased on both sides. Our squares and columns re-ascended the ridge in front of Starsiedel, and all the villagers hastened to leave their houses to rally each to their regiment. Ours was mixed up with two or three others, and when the divisions "ordered arms" in front of Kaya, we could hardly distinguish which was which.

Our company was then called over; there remained only forty-two men: the tall Fürst and Seger were no longer there; but Zébédé, Klipfel, and I had come out scot-free.

Unfortunately it was not over yet, for these Prussians, filled with insolence on account of our retreat, were already making new dispositions to attack us at Kaya. Masses of reinforcements arrived, the sight of which made me think that, for a great general, the Emperor had had a very bad idea in extending his army over Leipzig and letting us be surprised by more than a hundred thousand men.

Just as we were proceeding to re-form behind the division, Brenier and eighteen thousand old soldiers of the Prussian guard ascended the ridge at a run, carrying the shakos of our dead on their bayonets in sign of victory. At the same time the combat was prolonged on the left between Klein-Gorschen and Starsiedel. The mass of Russian cavalry that we had seen glitter in the sun that morning behind the Gonna-Bach, sought to drive us back; but the 6th corps had come up to cover us, and the regiments of marines stood like walls. The whole plain seemed but one cloud, where casques, cuirasses, and lances gleamed in thousands.

On our side we kept always retreating, when all on a

sudden something passed before us like a thunder-bolt —it was Marshal Ney; he came up at full gallop, followed by his staff. I never saw such a countenance: his eyes flamed, his cheeks quivered with rage! In a second he had passed along the whole line, and was at the head of our columns. All followed him as if drawn by a magic force: instead of retreating, we marched to meet the Prussians; ten minutes after, the air seemed on fire. But the enemy stood firm; they thought themselves already conquerors, and would not let go the victory: all the more because they were constantly receiving reinforcements, while we were quite exhausted by five hours' fighting.

Our battalion, this time, was in the second line, and the bullets passed over us; but a much worse noise, which shook my nerves more, was the rattle of the grape among the bayonets: it hissed like a kind of dreadful music and was heard far off. Amidst shouts, commands, and firing, we began to descend again on a heap of corpses. Our first divisions re-entered Klein-Gorschen; the fight was there hand-to-hand: in the village street nothing was to be seen but the butt ends of muskets in the air, and generals on horseback sword in hand like common soldiers.

This lasted some time; we said in the ranks, "That's right! we're advancing!" But new troops having come up on the Prussian side, we were obliged to retreat a second time, and unfortunately so quick, that a great number escaped into Kaya. This village was on the ridge, and the last before the road to Lutzen. It is a long narrow lane of houses separated from each other by little gardens, stables, and beehives. If the enemy attacked us at Kaya, the army would be cut in two.

As I fled, I recalled those words of M. Goulden, "If by mischance the allies beat us, they will come to revenge themselves on us in our own country for all we have been doing to them these ten years!" I thought the battle lost, for Marshal Ney himself, in the centre of a square, retreated, while the soldiers, coming out of the mêlée, carried off the wounded officers on litters formed by their muskets. Altogether things were going ill.

I entered Kaya on the right hand, striding over hedges and jumping the little palisades which divided the gardens. I was turning the corner of a shed, when, raising my head, I perceived about fifty officers on horseback halting at the top of a hill in front;

further off, behind them, masses of artillery were hastening at full speed on the road to Leipzig. This made me look, and I recognized the Emperor, a little in front of the others; he was seated, as in an arm chair, on his white horse. I saw him distinctly under the pale sky; he never stirred, but watched the battle below with his spy-glass.

This sight made me so joyful that I began to shout "Vive l'Empereur!" with all my might; then I entered the main street of Kaya, by a passage between two old houses. I was one of the first, and I perceived the villagers, men, women, and children, hastening to take refuge in their cellars.

Several people to whom I have related this, have reproached me for having run so fast; but I have answered them that when Michael Ney fled, Joseph Bertha might well fly too.

Klipfel, Zébédé, Sergeant Pinto, all whom I knew in the company, were still without, and I heard a most frightful noise going on. Columns of smoke soared above the roofs, tiles rolled and fell into the streets, and the cannon-balls knocked in the walls or broke the beams with a horrible din.

On all sides, by the lanes, above the hedges and

garden palisades, our soldiers entered with furious looks, turning at the same time to fire. There they were, from all regiments, without shakos, their uniforms torn, covered with blood; and, now that I think of it after so many years, they were all mere children: out of fifteen or twenty, scarcely one had moustaches; but courage is native in the French race!

The Prussians—led by old officers, who cried "Vorwärts! vorwärts!"—came on, climbing as it were over each other to get on quicker; while we, in the corner of a barn, twenty or thirty in number, in front of a garden where were beehives and large cherry-trees in flower, began a rolling fire on these rascals who tried to scale a low wall and take the village.

Hundreds of balls whistled in our ears and were flattened against the stones: the mortar fell, the thatch hung from the beams, the great gate to the left was shattered; and we, behind the barn, just ran forward to fire into the mass after having re-loaded. This took us only just the time requisite to aim and draw the trigger, and yet five or six had already fallen in the corner of the hayloft with their faces to the earth; but our rage was so great that we took no notice of it.

As I was turning for the tenth time, the musket fell

from my hand; I stooped to pick it up and fell upon it: I had a ball in my left shoulder and the blood flowed out upon my breast like warm water. I tried to raise myself, but all that I could do was to seat myself against the wall; the blood then ran down upon my thighs, and I began to think that I should die in this place: an idea which chilled me all over.

My comrades meanwhile kept on firing over my head, and the Prussians replying. Bethinking myself that another ball might finish me; with my right hand I pressed so hard against the corner of the wall to push myself away, that I fell into a little ditch which conveyed the water from the street into the garden. My left arm was heavy as lead and my head swam; I heard the firing still, but as in a dream. This must have lasted some time.

When I re-opened my eyes, the night was coming on; the Prussians filled the village, and in the garden in front was an old general, grey-haired, his head bare, on a great brown horse, calling with a voice like a trumpet, for the guns to be brought up. Near him, on the little wall loaded with corpses, a surgeon stood, and bound up his arm. Behind him, also on horseback, was a Russian officer, a very slender young man, wearing a hat with a cluster of drooping green plumes. I saw all in a moment; the old man with his hooked nose, his large, flat forehead, his eager eyes and fearless air; the others around him; the surgeon, a little, bald man in spectacles; and five or six hundred paces off, our soldiers re-forming between two houses.

There was now no more firing; but between Klein-Gorschen and Kaya, fearful cries arose, mixed with the noise of heavily-rolling wheels, neighing of horses, swearing, and cracking of whips, and then two sixteen-pounders, drawn each by six horses, turned the corner into the street. The artillerymen lashed the horses furiously, and the wheels drove into the heaps of dead and wounded as into so much straw: the bones cracked! and thence came the loud cries I had heard.

"Here!" cried the old man in German, "aim down there, between the two houses." Then, as he entered the street again, I heard him say to the young Russian officer,

"Tell the Emperor Alexander that I am in Kaya. The battle is won if they but send me reinforcements. Let them not parley—but *do* it! We must look for a furious assault. Napoleon is coming—I am sure of it! In half-an-hour we shall have him with his Guard. Cost what it may, I'll make a stand against him. But in God's name, let them not lose a minute: then the victory is ours!"

The young man galloped off and I heard some one say, "That old fellow is Blucher! . . . Ah, scoundrel, if I had but my musket!"

I turned and saw an old sergeant, a dry, spare figure, with wrinkled cheeks, seated against the barn door, his hands resting on the ground to support himself, for he had a ball in the back. His yellow eyes followed the Prussian general with a sinister gaze; his hooked nose curved like a beak on his long moustaches: he had a haughty menacing look.

I meanwhile thought that I should, perhaps, be buried next day with all the others in the garden opposite, and tears ran down my cheeks. The sergeant looked sideways at me, and seeing me still so young, asked me—

"What have *you* got, conscript?"

"A ball in the shoulder, sergeant!"

"In the shoulder; that's better than in the back. You may get rid of it!"

And looking at me again with a softer voice, he said—

"Don't be afraid—*you'll* see your country again."

The sergeant said no more; only from time to time he made an effort to raise his head and see if our column were coming. He swore between his teeth, and finally let himself slip to the ground, still leaning against the door, and saying, "My business is done!—that big rascal has paid me, however."

He looked into the hedge opposite, where lay stretched on his back a Prussian grenadier, his bayonet across him.

It must have been about ten o'clock. I felt cold all over, and was sitting benumbed, my face on my knees, when the rumbling of cannon woke me up anew. The battery of eighty-four pieces which the Emperor had ordered up, made a fearful din, in spite of the distance: the old shed against which I leaned, shook to its foundation.

At last, in about twenty minutes, the Prussians and Russians began to retire; re-passing in crowds by the narrow passage where we were. The cries of "Vive l'Empereur!" drew nearer. I felt a hand grasp me by the arm; I turned and saw the old sergeant, half-dead, but looking at me, and laughing grimly. The roof of our shed gave way and the wall tottered, but we took no heed: we only saw the defeat of our enemies, and only heard, amid all this horrible din, the shouts, ever nearer and nearer, of our soldiers.

Suddenly the sergeant, growing quite pale, exclaimed, "There he is!"

And bending forward on his knees, with one hand on the earth, the other raised, he cried in a loud, clear voice,—

"Vive l'Empereur!"

Then he fell with his face on the earth and never stirred more!

I too bent forward to see, and caught sight of Napoleon riding amidst the firing, his hat drawn down over his large head, his grey surtout open, a broad red ribbon across his white waistcoat; he looking calm, and cold, as if lighted by the reflection of the bayonets. All gave way before him; the Prussian gunners abandoned their pieces, and leapt over the garden wall, in spite of their officers who strove to retain them.

These things which I saw, are painted as in fire on my mind; but from that moment I remember no more of the battle, for whilst rejoicing in the hope of our victory, I lost consciousness and lay like one dead amongst the dead.

CHAPTER XIV.

I AWAKENED again in the night amidst the silence. Clouds traversed the sky, and the moon looked down on the forsaken village, the overthrown cannons and the heap of dead, as she has looked down since the beginning of the world on the flow of water, the growing of grass, and the fall of leaves in autumn. Men are nothing beside eternal things. Those who are going to die understand this better than others.

I could no longer stir, and I suffered much: my right arm only had power to move. However, I managed to raise myself on my elbow, and I saw the dead heaped up the whole length of the street. The moon shone upon them overhead, and their faces were white as snow; some lay with their mouths and eyes wide open, others with their faces to the earth, their cartridge-boxes and knapsacks on their backs, their hands gripping their muskets. It was a frightful sight to see.

I tried to call for help. I heard only what sounded like the weak cry of a sobbing child, and I gave myself up to despair. But this feeble cry that I had uttered in the silence, exciting others more or less near, caused the sound to spread on all sides. All the wounded thought they heard aid arriving, and those who could still make a sound, called too. These cries lasted some instants; then all was still. I heard only a horse breathing slowly near me behind the hedge: he tried to rise: I saw his head lifted at the end of his long neck, then he fell back again.

As for me, by the effort I had just made, my wound was re-opened, and I felt the blood trickling anew under my arm. Then I closed my eyes to let myself die; and everything far off, from the time of my first infancy—everything in the village, when my poor mother held me in her arms and sang me to sleep—the little bedroom, the old alcove, our dog Powner who played with me and rolled me over on the ground, my father who came in so gaily in the evening, his axe on his shoulder, and took me in his large hands to kiss me—all these things returned on me as in a dream!

I thought, "Ah, poor mother! poor father! if you had known that you were bringing up your child with such love and care, that he might one day perish miserably, alone, far from your help, what would not have been your wretchedness and your maledictions against those who had reduced him to such a state. Ah, if you were here! If I could only ask your forgiveness for the trouble I have caused you!"

At this thought my breast heaved, and the tears bathed my face. Then came the thought of Catherine, Aunt Grédel, and good M. Goulden; and this was something dreadful! I saw their astonishment and their tears at hearing of a great battle. Aunt Grédel, who ran every day along the road to go to the post, while Catherine waited for her, praying, and M. Goulden, alone in his room, reading in the gazette that the 3rd corps had lost more than the others. He walked alone with his head bent down, and came very late to seat himself, all absently, at the counter. My spirit was there with them: it waited in a manner at the post with Aunt Grédel; it returned dejected to the village, and saw Catherine in her wretchedness.

Then I seemed to see the postman, Rœdig, calling at Quatre Vents one morning, with his blouse and his little leather bag. He opened the house door, and held out a large paper to Aunt Grédel, who remained transfixed, while Catherine stood beside her pale as death. It was the notification of my death just arrived! I heard the piercing sobs of Catherine, stretched on the ground, and the imprecations of Aunt Grédel, her grey hair all loose, crying that there was no more justice on earth. The good M. Goulden came to console them; but as soon as he entered, he began to sob too, and all cried out, "Oh, poor Joseph! poor Joseph!"

It tore my heart. And then too it seemed to me that thirty or forty thousand families in France, in Russia, in Germany, were soon to receive the same news; and, more dreadful still, a great number of the poor fellows stretched on the battle-field had still their fathers and mothers. I pictured this to myself as an abomination—a great cry of the human race mounting to heaven.

Then I recalled those poor women of Phalsbourg, who were praying in the church at the dreadful retreat from Russia, and I understood what passed in their hearts! . . . I thought how Catherine would soon be going there; that she would pray for years and years thinking of me. Yes, I thought that; for I knew that we had loved each other from our infancy, and that she could never forget me. My emotion was so great that one tear followed another down my cheeks: and yet it did me good to have this confidence in her, and to be sure that she would preserve her love even up to old age—that she would always have me before her eyes, and that she would never take another.

The dew had begun to fall towards the morning. I thought of God, who from the beginning of time has made the same things, and whose power is without bounds, who pardons faults, because He is good; and I hoped that He would pardon me in consideration of my sufferings.

From time to time I heard a wall fall in the village, and a roof sink down. The animals, scared by the fighting, had regained confidence, and came out at daybreak: a goat bleated in the neighbouring stall, a great shepherd's dog, with his tail drooping, passed by, looking at the corpses; the horse began to snort terribly, taking him perhaps for a wolf, and the dog ran away.

All these details return to me, because at the moment of dying one sees and hears everything: one says to oneself as it were, "Look, listen, for soon you will hear and see no more in this world!"

But what remains far more deeply in my mind, and which I shall never forget if I should live a hundred years, is when from afar I thought I heard the sound of voices. Oh, how I aroused myself—how I listened, and raised myself up on my arm to cry, "Help!" It was still night, though a little gleam of daylight began to streak the sky. Far off, across the rain which filled the air, a light moved amidst the fields; it went at random, stopping here and there, and then I saw dark forms bending around: they were not confused shadows, but others beside me also saw this light; for on all sides sighs rose into the night, plaintive cries, voices so feeble that one would have said they were little children calling their mother!

My God, what is this life? What is it made of that we should attach such value to it? This miserable breath which costs us all so much tears and sufferings, why do we more dread to lose it than anything else in the world? What is there reserved to us hereafter, since at the least fear of death one trembles all over?

Who knows? All men have spoken of this from age to age; all think of it, and no one can tell.

In my ardent desire to live, I gazed at this light, as a drowning wretch gazes at the shore: I struggled to see it, and my heart thrilled with hope. I tried to call out, but my voice went no further than my lips. The pattering of the rain in the trees and on the roofs drowned everything; yet in spite of that I said to myself, —"They hear me—they are coming!" I seemed to see the lantern move up the garden-path, and the light enlarge at every step; but after having wandered some instants on the battle-field, it entered slowly into a hollow of the ground and disappeared.

Then I fell back and lost all consciousness.

CHAPTER XV.

It was at the further end of a great shed in the form of a market, with pillars all round, that I returned to my senses; some one gave me wine and water to drink, and I found it very good. Opening my eyes, I saw an old soldier with grey moustaches, who was holding my head and putting the goblet to my lips.

"Well!" he said to me with an air of good humour, "well! you are better?"

And I could not help answering him with a smile at the thought that I was still living. I had my chest and left shoulder strongly bandaged; I felt as if they had been burned; but for all that I cared not—I was alive!

I began first to look at the great beams which crossed in the air, and the tiles, where the light entered in more than one place; then, after some instants, I turned my head, and I recognized that I was in one of those vast sheds where the brewers of the country shelter their barrels and their carriages. All around, on mattresses and trusses of straw, were ranged a crowd of the wounded, and in the middle, on a great kitchen-table, a surgeon-major and his two aides, with shirt-sleeves up, were cutting off some man's leg; the wounded man was groaning. Behind them was a heap of legs and arms, and the ideas that they excited in me may be imagined.

Five or six infantry soldiers gave the wounded drink; they had jugs and cups.

But what made most impression on me, was this surgeon in shirt-sleeves, who cut on and heeded nothing; he had a large nose, hollow cheeks, and every minute scolded his aides, who were not quick enough in giving him knives, forceps, lint, linen, or who did not at once sponge up the blood. It was not badly done, however, for in less than a quarter of an hour they had cut off two legs.

Outside, against the pillars, was stationed a great carriage full of straw.

Just as they had placed on the table a Russian carbinier, at least six feet high, whose neck was pierced by a ball near the ear, another surgeon passed before the shed: a cavalry-surgeon, short, fat, and much pitted with the small-pox; he had a portfolio under his arm, and stepped near the carriage.

"Ha! Forel!" he cried gaily.

"Why, it's you, Duchêne!" replied our surgeon, turning round. "How many wounded?"

"From seventeen to eighteen thousand."

"Diable!—Is that going on this morning?"

"Yes, to be sure; I am going to look for linen."

Our doctor came out of the shed to shake hands with his comrade, and they began to chat quietly, while the aides took a draught of wine, and the Russian rolled his eyes with a look of despair.

"Look here, Duchêne, you've only got to go down the street—fronting this wall—you see? Just in front, you'll find the canteen."

"Ah, very good, thank you. I'm off!"

So off he went, and our surgeon called after him,—

"A good appetite to you, Duchêne!"

Then he returned to the side of his expectant Russian, and began by opening his neck from the nape to the shoulder. He worked with an air of ill-humour, saying to the aides,—

"Come, gentlemen, look sharp!"

The Russian sighed, as may be imagined; but he paid no attention, and finally throwing a bullet on the ground, he put on a bandage, and said—"Take him away!"

The Russian was taken off the table, the soldiers laid him on a mattress, in a row with others, and his neighbour was brought.

Five or six mattresses off from mine was seated an old corporal, with a bandaged leg; he winked his eye and said to his neighbour, whose arm had just been cut off,—

"Conscript, first look into that heap; I wager you won't have your own arm again."

The other, who, though very pale, had yet shown the greatest courage, looked, and almost immediately lost all consciousness.

Then the corporal began to laugh, and said—

"He recognised it at last. . . . It's that one underneath, with a little blue flower. . . . It always produces that effect."

He seemed to admire himself for having discovered this; but nobody laughed with him. The wounded cried at every minute,—

"Some drink!" When one began, all followed:

the old soldier had no doubt taken a fancy to me, for always in passing he presented his cup to me.

I did not remain there more than an hour; ten other carriages had come up, and been ranged behind the first. Some peasants, in velvet jackets and large black hats, with whip on shoulder, waited, holding their horses by the bridle. A picket of hussars presently arrived, the quartermaster dismounted, and coming into the shed, said,—

"Beg pardon, major, but here's an order to escort twelve carriages full of wounded to Lutzen; are they to be loaded here?"

"Yes, here," said the surgeon; and all at once they began to load the first row. The peasants and the ambulance men, before taking us away, made us drink a good draught of wine. As soon as one carriage was full, it started, and another drew up. I was in the third, seated on the straw, in a front row, beside a conscript of the twenty-seventh, who had lost his right hand; behind, another was without one leg, another had his head cleft, another his jaw broken, and so on till the end.

Our great coats were given back to us; yet we were so cold, in spite of the sun, that nothing but our noses, our foraging caps, and the linen bandages above the collars, could be seen. No one spoke: we had enough to think of for ourselves.

From time to time I felt a dreadful chill, then all of a sudden gusts of heat, which came into my very eyes: it was the beginning of a fever. But on starting from Kaya there was still nothing much amiss; I saw everything clearly, and it was only afterwards, when near Leipzig, that I felt altogether ill.

At last we were all packed after this fashion; those who could still keep themselves up, seated in the foremost carriages, the others stretched out in the hindmost ones; and so we started. The hussars, on horseback near us, talked about the battle, smoked and laughed, without looking at us.

It was in traversing Kaya that I saw all the horrors of war. The village consisted now of nothing but a heap of ruins. The roofs had fallen; only the gables here and there remained upright; the beams and laths were broken, and one saw through them the little chambers with their alcoves, their doors, and their staircases. Poor people, women, children, and old men, went and came in the houses in despair; they ascended and descended the stairs as if in cages in the open air.

Sometimes, high up, the fireplace of a little room with a little mirror and branches of box over it, showed that there in the time of peace a young girl had lived.

Ah! who could then foresee that one day all this happiness would be destroyed, not by the fury of the winds or the anger of the heavens, but by the rage of men, still more formidable?

There was nothing, down to the poor animals, that had not a deserted look amidst these ruins: the pigeons sought their pigeon-house, and the oxen and goats their stalls; the poor beasts went comfortless through the alleys, lowing and bellowing plaintively; fowls were perched on the trees, and everywhere—everywhere we saw the traces of bullets.

At the last house, a white-haired old man, seated on the threshold of his ruined dwelling, held a little child on his knees; he looked at us as we passed with a mournful and gloomy air. Did he see us? I know not; but his forehead ploughed with deep wrinkles and his haggard eyes announced despair. What years of labour, what economies and sufferings it had cost him to secure the repose of his old age! Now all was destroyed; the child and he had no longer a roof to shelter their heads!

And these trenches half a league long, where the country people toiled in haste to prevent a pestilence from completing the destruction of the human race! I saw them, also, from the top of the hill of Kaya, and turned my eyes away with horror! Yes, I have seen these immense trenches, in which were interred the dead—Russians, French, Prussians, all pell-mell, as God had made them to love each other, before the invention of plumes and uniforms, which divide them for the advantage of those who govern them. They are there — they embrace — and if something lives again in them, which one must needs hope, they love and pardon each other — cursing the crime which, from age to age, prevents them from being brothers till after death!

But what was still more mournful was the long string of carriages conveying away the wounded: those poor wretches who are only spoken of in the bulletins to diminish their number, and who perish in the hospital like flies, far from all those whom they love, while cannons are fired and hymns sung in churches in joyful commemoration of the slaughter of thousands of men!

When we arrived at Lutzen, the town was so encumbered with the wounded, that our convoy received orders to start for Leipzig. We saw in the streets nothing but poor fellows three-quarters dead, stretched along under the houses on straw. It took us more than an hour to reach a church, where were left fifteen or twenty who could no longer bear the journey.

The quartermaster and his men, after having refreshed in a public-house at a corner of the *Place*, remounted on horseback, and we continued on our way to Leipzig.

Then I saw and heard no more; my head turned, my ears tingled, I took trees for men, and I felt a thirst which can hardly be imagined. Others in the carriages had for a long while been shrieking and raving, talking of their mothers, trying to rise and jump out on the road! I know not if I did the same; but I woke as from a bad dream, at the moment when two men took me each by one leg and each with an arm round my body, and carried me across a gloomy *Place*. The sky was crowded with stars, and on the façade of a great building which stood out black amidst the night, glittered innumerable lights; it was the hospital of the Faubourg of Halle, at Leipzig.

The two men ascended a winding stair, and at the top they entered an immense hall, where from one end to the other extended beds in three rows almost touching each other, in one of which I was laid. The shrieks, oaths, and moans heard there, are not to be imagined; all these hundreds of wounded men had the fever. The windows were open, and the little lanterns quivered in the current of air. Hospital nurses, doctors, and aides with their long aprons tied under their arms, went and came. And the deep hum of the halls below, the people ascending and descending, the new convoys unloading in the *Place*, the shouts of the drivers, the cracking of whips, the stamping of the horses—all continued to bewilder one's brain.

Then for the first time, while they were undressing me, I felt such a horrible pain in my shoulder that I could not refrain from crying out. A surgeon arrived almost immediately, and reproached my attendants for their neglect. This was all that I remember of that night; for I was like a maniac: I called Catherine, M. Goulden, and Aunt Grédel to my aid—as I was afterwards told by my neighbour, an old horse artilleryman, whom my ravings hindered from sleeping.

It was not till the next morning, about eight o'clock, at the first dressing of my wound, that I saw the hall clearly. Then too I knew that the bone of my left shoulder was broken.

When I awoke I was in the midst of a dozen surgeons; one of them, a large swarthy man, whom they called "M. le Baron," was opening the bandages; an aide at the foot of my bed held a basin of warm water. The principal examined my wound: all the others leant forward to hear what he was going to say. He spoke to them for some instants, but all that I could comprehend was that the ball had gone upwards, that it had broken the bone and come out behind. I saw that he understood his business, since the Prussians had fired low, over the garden walls, and that the ball must needs have re-ascended. He washed the wound himself, and replaced the bandage in a turn or two of the hand, so that my shoulder could not move, and everything was in order.

I felt myself much better. Ten minutes after, a hospital nurse came to change my shirt, which, by dint of practice, he did without hurting me. The surgeon had stopped beside the other bed and said,—

"Ah, there you are again, old fellow!"

"Yes, Monsieur le Baron, here I am," answered

the gunner, quite proud to see himself recognised: "the first time was at Austerlitz, for a grape-shot wound, then at Jena, then at Smolensk for two lance wounds."

"Ay, ay," said the surgeon, seemingly moved "and now what have we got?"

"Three sabre-wounds on the left arm while defending my piece against the Prussian hussars."

The surgeon approached, undid the bandage, and I heard him ask the gunner—

"You've got the cross?"

"No, Monsieur le Baron."

"What's your name?"

"Christian Zimmer, quartermaster of the 3rd regiment of horse artillery."

"Very good! very good!"

He dressed the wounds, saying as he rose, "They will do well!" then turned away, talking with the others, and went out after completing his rounds and giving some orders to the nurses.

The old gunner appeared quite delighted. As I had just discovered from his name that he came from Alsace, I began to speak to him in our language, which gladdened him still more.

He was a fine man of six feet high, with round

shoulders, flat forehead, large nose, *moustaches* of a reddish blonde; he was hard as a rock, but a good fellow all the same. His eyes wrinkled up and his ears pricked up when one spoke Alsatian to him: I might have asked him for anything in Alsatian, he would have given me all, if he had had anything; but he had only a grasp of the hand, which made one's bones crack. He called me *Josephel*, after the fashion in our country, and said to me—

"*Josephel*, beware of swallowing all the remedies they give you . . . . Don't swallow anything you don't know . . . Whatever doesn't smell nice is worth nothing. If they gave us every day a bottle of Rike-vir we should soon be cured; but it's more convenient to demolish our stomachs with a handful of weeds boiled in water, than to bring us white Alsace."

When I was frightened about the fever, and at what I saw, he put on a displeased air, and looking at me with his large grey eyes, said—

"*Josephel*, are you so crazy as to be frightened? Do you think such stout fellows as we can die in a hospital? No, no, put that idea out of your head."

But say what he would, every morning the doctors, making their rounds, found seven or eight of us dead.

Some caught a burning fever, some a chill, and it always ended with the bier, which we saw pass on the shoulders of the nurses! So that one never knew whether it was best to be hot or cold.

Zimmer said to me, "All this, *Josephel*, comes from the noxious drugs which the doctors invent. Do you see that tall thin fellow? He can boast of having killed more men than any one field-piece. He is as it were always loaded with grape, with a lighted match. And that little black man! Were I the Emperor, I would send him to the Prussians and Russians: he would kill more men than a corps of soldiers."

I could easily have been made to laugh at these pleasantries, if I had not seen the biers pass.

By the end of three weeks the bone of my shoulder began to be set, the two wounds gradually closed, and I scarcely suffered any more. The sabre wounds that Zimmer had on his arms and shoulder also went on very well. Every morning we had good broth, which strengthened our hearts, and in the evening a little beef, with half a glass of wine, the mere sight of which gladdened us and made us see the future in a cheerful light.

About this time we were also permitted to descend

into a great garden full of old elms, behind the hospital. There were benches under the trees, and we walked about in the alleys just as if we were the owners, in large grey cloaks and cotton caps.

It was a magnificent season. Our view extended over the Partha, bordered with poplars. This river falls into the Elster, to the left, forming long blue lines. In the same direction extends a forest of beeches, and in the foreground pass three or four broad white roads, which traverse fields of wheat, barley, oats, and hop plantations: in fact, everything agreeable and rich that one can possibly imagine; especially when the wind blows upon it, and all these harvests bend and then rise again in the sunshine.

The heat of the month of June announced a good year. Often, seeing this beautiful country, I thought of Phalsbourg and began to weep. Zimmer said to me,—

"I should like to know why the devil you cry, *Josephel?* Instead of having caught the hospital fever, or having lost an arm or a leg, like hundreds of others, here we are peaceably seated on a bench in the shade; we get both meat and wine; we are allowed to smoke, when we have tobacco—and you are not contented! What is there you are in want of?"

Then I told him of my love affair with Catherine, my walks to Quatre-vents, our vain hopes, our promise of marriage: in short, of all that happy time which was now only a dream. He listened, smoking his pipe.

"Ay, ay," he said, "'tis sad enough, no doubt. Before the conscription of 1798, I also was to have married a girl of our village named Margrédel, whom I loved like my own eyes. We had given each other our promise, and through all the campaign of Zurich, I never passed a day without thinking of Margrédel. Well, as soon as ever I get leave, I go to my country, and what do I learn? That she had been married three months to a shoemaker in our place named Passauf.

"You may imagine my anger, *Josephel;* I could see nothing clearly. I wanted to destroy everybody, and as they told me that Passauf was at the brewery of the *Grand Cerf,* I went there without looking right or left. Arriving, I recognized him at the end of the table, near a window looking into the yard, against the pump. He was laughing with two or three other scamps, who were all drinking together. I approached, and he called out,— 'Why, there's Christian Zimmer? How are you, Christian? Margrédel desires her compliments to you.' He winked as he spoke. I immediately seized hold of a jug and broke it on his left ear, saying, 'Go and give her that from me, Passauf; 'tis my wedding present.' Of course all the others fell upon me; I knocked down two or three more with a pitcher, mounted on a table, got out of a window into the *Place*, and escaped.

"Scarcely had I come home to my mother than the *gendarmerie* arrived, and arrested me by order of the authorities. They tied me on a cart, and took me back from brigade to brigade to my regiment, which was at Strasbourg. I remained six weeks at Finckmatt, and should, perhaps, have had to drag a cannon-ball, if we had not passed the Rhine to go to Hohenlinden. Commandant Courtaud himself said to me,—'You can boast of taking good aim, 'tis true, but if you're caught knocking down people with a jug any more, 'twill be the worse for you. I warn you. Is that the proper way of fighting, brute? Why do we wear a sabre, if not to make use of it and do honour to our country?' I had not a word to say in reply.

"From that time, *Josephel*, the taste for marriage left me. Don't talk to me of a soldier who is thinking about his wife—it's contemptible. Look at those generals who are married, do they fight as they used?

Not they: they have but one idea; it is to increase their fortunes, and especially to enjoy them, living comfortably with their duchesses and their little dukes by their firesides. My grandfather, Yeri, the forester, always said that a good sporting dog ought to be thin, and, putting aside difference of rank, I think the same of good generals and good soldiers. *We* are always under orders; but our generals get fat, and that comes of the good dinners at their own houses."

So spoke Zimmer in the sincerity of his heart; but that did not prevent me from being sad.

As soon as I was able to get up, I had hastened to inform M. Goulden by letter that I was at the hospital of Halle, in one of the faubourgs of Leipzig, with a slight wound in the arm; but that there was nothing to be feared for me, for that I got regularly better. I begged him to show my letter to Catherine and Aunt Grédel, in order to give them confidence in the midst of this terrible war. I told him, too, that my greatest happiness would be to receive news from my country and of the health of those whom I loved.

From that moment I had no more rest; every morning I looked for an answer, and to see the quartermaster distribute twenty or thirty letters to all the hall without my receiving one, pierced me to the heart: I went down quickly into the garden to hide my tears. There was a dark corner where broken pots were thrown—a place covered with shade, which pleased me best, because the rest never came there. Here I passed my time dreaming, on an old mouldy bench. I was haunted by dark ideas: I went so far as to believe that Catherine could forget her promise, and I cried to myself,—"Ah! if only I had been left at Kaya, all would have been over! . . . . Why did they not abandon me? That would have been better than suffering so much."

Things had come to such a pass that I wished not to be cured, when one morning the quartermaster, amongst the other names, called that of Joseph Bertha; I raised my hand without being able to speak, and a great square letter, covered with innumerable stamps, was given me. I recognized M. Goulden's handwriting, which turned me quite pale.

"Well," said Zimmer, laughing, "it comes after all, you see."

I made no answer; but, when I was dressed, I crammed the letter into my pocket, and ran down to read it alone in the place to which I always went, at the bottom of the garden. On opening it, I saw two or three little apple-blossoms, which I took out, and a money order, with a few words from M. Goulden. But it was not that which touched me most, and which made me tremble from head to foot—it was Catherine's writing, which I looked at with dim eyes, unable to read it, my heart beat so powerfully.

However, I managed to calm myself a little, and quietly read my letter; stopping from time to time to make sure that I did not deceive myself—that it was really my dear Catherine who wrote to me, and that I was not in a dream.

This letter I have kept, because it in a manner restored me to life: here it is, such as I received it, on the 8th of June, 1813.

"My dear Joseph,—

"This letter is to tell you, to begin with, that I love you always more and more, and that I shall never love any one but you. You will know, also, that my greatest grief is to know that you are wounded in a hospital, and that I cannot take care of you. It is a very great grief; and since the departure of the conscripts we have not had an hour's peace. My mother was displeased, saying that I was silly to cry day and night; but she cried as much as I, all alone in the evening at the hearth: I heard her quite well from upstairs; and her anger fell upon Pinacle, who dared no longer go to the market, because she had a hammer in her basket.

"But our greatest grief of all, Joseph, was when the rumour ran that a battle had just been fought, where thousands and thousands of men had been killed. We were scarcely alive; my mother ran every morning to the post, and I could not stir from my bed. At last, at last your letter *did* come. Now I am better, I can weep freely, blessing God who has saved your life.

"And when I think how happy we were once, Joseph, when you came every Sunday, and we remained seated near each other without stirring, and thinking of nothing! Ah! we did not know our happiness; we did not know what might happen to us! But God's will be done! If only you are cured, we may hope once more to be together as we were. Many people talk of peace; but we have had so many misfortunes, and the Emperor Napoleon is so fond of war, that one can no longer trust to anything.

"All that gives me pleasure is to know that your wound is not dangerous, and that you love me still. . . . . Oh, Joseph, I shall love you for ever! I can say nothing else—it is all that I can say to you from the bottom of my heart, and I know that my mother loves you well.

"Now M. Goulden wishes to write you a few words. I embrace you a thousand and a thousand times. The weather is beautiful here; we shall have a fine year. The great apple-tree in the orchard is all white with blossoms; I am going to gather some to put into the letter for you, when M. Goulden has written: perhaps by God's grace we shall once more eat some of those fine apples together. Embrace me as I embrace you; and adieu, adieu, Joseph!"

I melted into tears while reading, and Zimmer coming up, I said,—

"Come, sit down, and I will read you what my sweetheart writes to me; you will see then if she is a Margrédel."

"Just let me light my pipe," he said. He did so, and added, "You may begin, *Josephel;* but I warn you myself, I am an old stager: I don't believe all that people write; women are more cunning than we."

In spite of this I read him Catherine's letter slowly. He said nothing, and when I had done, he took it and looked at it a long time with a musing air; then he gave it back to me, saying,—

"There, *Josephel;* 'tis a good girl, full of good sense, and who will never take another than you."

"You think she really loves me?"

"Yes, she's one you may trust to: *she*'ll never marry a Passauf. I would sooner distrust the Emperor than such a girl."

I could have embraced Zimmerman for those words, and I said to him,—

"I have received from home a note of a hundred francs, which we can get cashed at the post. The principal thing is to have white wine. Let us try to get out from here."

"A good idea," said he, turning up his long moustaches, and putting his pipe back into his pocket. "I don't like to moulder in a garden when there are public-houses outside. We must try to get leave."

We rose joyously and ascended the hospital stairs, when the quartermaster coming down, stopped Zimmer, asking him,—

"Do you happen to be one Christian Zimmer, gunner to the 2nd Horse Artillery?"

"By your leave, quartermaster, I have that honour."

"Well, here's something for you," he said, handing him a small packet and a large letter.

Zimmer was stupefied, having never received anything before from home or elsewhere. He opened the packet, in which was a box, then he opened the box, and saw the Cross of the Legion of Honour! he turned quite pale, his eyes grew dim for an instant, he rested his hand on the balustrade behind him; but presently he cried, "*Vive* l'Empereur!" in so tremendous a voice, that the three halls re-echoed it.

The quartermaster looked at him with complacency. "You are content?"

"Content, quartermaster? I should think so. I want only one thing more."

"What?"

"Leave to take a turn in the town."

"You must apply to M. Tardieu, the chief surgeon."

He went down laughing, and as it was the visiting-hour, we went up, arm-in-arm, to ask leave of the chief surgeon, a grey-headed old man, who had heard the shout of "Vive l'Empereur!" and looked gravely at us.

"What's the matter?" he said.

Zimmer showed him his cross, and said,—

"Beg pardon, doctor; but I feel as strong as a lion!"

"I believe you," said M. Tardieu. "You want an order to go out?"

"If you *would* be so good—for me and my comrade Joseph Bertha."

The surgeon had examined my wound overnight; he drew from his pocket a portfolio, and gave us two orders. We went down again, proud as kings: Zimmer of his cross of honour, I of my letter.

Below in the great vestibule the concièrge cried out to us,—

"Well, well! where are you going?"

Zimmer showed him our orders, and we went forth, happy to breathe the outer air. A sentinel showed us the post-office, where I went to get my hundred francs. Then more serious—because our joy was a little subdued—we reached the gate of Halle, at twice musket-range on the left, at the end of a long lime avenue. Each faubourg is divided from the ancient ramparts by one of these lanes, and all round Leipzig runs another very wide avenue also, of lime trees. The ramparts are old buildings, such as one sees at Saint Hippolytes, in the Haut-Rhin—decrepit walls all grass-grown: unless, indeed, the Germans have repaired them since 1813.

CHAPTER XVI.

How many things we had to learn that day! In the hospital, nobody troubles himself about anything; when one sees every morning the wounded men come in by fifties, and sees so many go out every evening on a bier, it shows one the world in miniature, and one thinks, "The world will last our time."

But outside, ideas change. Beholding the main-street of Halle—that old city, with its magazines and portes cochères encumbered with merchandise; those old roofs projecting like outhouses; those large, low waggons with piled-up bales of goods; in short, all the whole spectacle of active commercial life, I was astonished. I had never seen the like, and I thought to myself, "Here is truly a trading town such as they are represented to us, full of industrious inhabitants, seeking to gain their livelihood, ease, and riches; where each one wishes to rise, not to the detriment of others, but by labouring hard, by devising day and night the means of prosperity for his family: which does not hinder all the world from profiting by inventions and discoveries. That's the happiness of peace in the midst of a dreadful war!"

And, meanwhile, it gave me pain to see the poor wounded men, who came forth with arm in a sling or limping and supported on crutches. I let myself be led, all in a reverie, by my friend Zimmer, who recognized every corner of a street, and said to me, "There, that's the Church of St. Nicholas; that's the great building of the university; that's the Hotel de Ville."

He remembered everything, having already seen Leipzig in 1807, before the battle of Friedland, and never ceased to repeat to me: "We are here as at Metz, at Strasbourg, or anywhere in France: the people are our friends. After the campaign of 1806, every politeness that could be shown *was* shown us. The citizens had us to dine with them, three and four at a time. They called us the heroes of Jena. You'll see now how fond they are of us! Enter where we will, everywhere they'll receive us as the benefactors of the country; it's we who made their elector King of Saxony, and we gave them, too, a good slice of Poland."

All at once Zimmer stopped before a little, low door, exclaiming,—

"Why, that's the Mouton d'Or beer-house; the façade fronts the other street, but we can enter this way. Come along!"

I followed him into a species of crooked passage, which soon led us to the end of an old court surrounded by high mud buildings, with little worm-eaten galleries under the gables, and the weather-cock above, as in the street of the Tosse-des-Janneurs, at Strasbourg. On the right was the beer-house; one could see the iron-hooped vats resting upon dark beams, heaps of hops and barley already boiled, and in a corner a great wheel with a winch, which an enormous dog kept in motion by running like a squirrel in a cage, pumping the beer at every turn.

The clink of glasses and pewter jugs was heard in the hall to the right, looking out on the Rue de Tilly, and, under the windows of this hall, opened a deep cellar, resounding with the cooper's hammer. The good smell of the new March beer filled the air, and Zimmer, his eyes raised to the roof, his face expanded with satisfaction, exclaimed,—

"Yes, 'tis here that we used to come: the tall Ferré,

the left-handed gunner, the big Rousillon, and I. God of heaven! how I rejoice at seeing all this again, *Josephel!* Why, it is six years ago that poor Rousillon. . . . his bones were laid last year at Smolensk; and Ferré must now be in his village near Toul, for his left leg was carried off at Wagram. How everything comes back when one thinks of it!"

Meanwhile he pushed open the door, and we entered a lofty hall full of smoke. It took me a few moments to see through this murky cloud a long row of tables surrounded with drinkers, most of them in short frock-coats and small caps, and the others in the Saxon uniform. There were students, young men of family, who came to Leipzig to study law, medicine, and all that can be learnt while emptying glasses and leading a jolly life, which they call *Fuchs commerz.* They often fight each other with a light sabre with sharp edges, but round at the end, so that they scar each other's faces, as Zimmer told me, but never endanger life. This shows the good sense of these students, who know well that life is a precious thing, and that it is better to have five or six scars, or even more, than to lose it.

Zimmer laughed while telling me this; he was blinded by his love of glory, and said you might as well load cannons with baked potatoes as fight duels with round-topped steel laths.

Finally, we entered the hall, and saw the eldest of these students—a tall, thin fellow, with hollow eyes, red nose, and a flaxen beard beginning to be stained yellow from being often dipped in beer—we saw him standing on a table and reading loud from a gazette, which hung from his right hand like an apron; in his left hand he held a long pipe.

All his companions, with their fair hair falling in curls on the collars of their short frock-coats, listened with their glasses in the air; just as we entered, we heard them repeating together, "*Vaterland! Vaterland!*" They drank healths with the Saxon soldiers, while the tall thin one stooped to take his glass too, and the stout brewer, with his grey, curly head, his snub nose, round eyes, and cheeks like pumpkins, cried with a thick voice, "Gesundheit! Gesundheit!"

"Come, come, comrades," cried Zimmer, "don't disturb yourselves; go on reading: we shan't be sorry, either, to learn the news."

But the young men would not profit by our invitation, and the eldest came down from the table, folding up his paper, and putting it in his pocket.

"It is done," he said.

"Yes, it is done," repeated the others, with a singular expression.

Two or three Saxon soldiers went out immediately, as if to take the air in the court, and disappeared. The big tavern-keeper said to us,—

"Perhaps you don't know that the great hall is on the Rue de Tilly side?"

"Oh, yes, we know it well," said Zimmer; "but I like this little hall best. It was here we used to come once on a time—two old comrades and I—to empty a few glasses in honour of Jena and Auerstadt. This hall recalls pleasant days to me."

"Ah! just as you please, just as you please," said the brewer. "You want March beer?"

"Yes, two tumblers, and the gazette."

"Very good!"

He served us, and Zimmer, who perceived nothing, tried to talk with the students, who excused themselves and went away one after the other. I felt that all these people bore us a hatred, all the more fearful that they dared not show it on the spot.

The gazette, which came from France, spoke of nothing but an armistice, after two new victories at

Bautzen and at Wurtschen. We then learnt that this armistice had begun on the 6th of June, and that conferences were being held at Prague in Bohemia to arrange a peace.

This of course gave me pleasure; I hoped they would send at least the lame ones home. But Zimmer, with his habit of saying everything out loud, filled the hall with his comments; he interrupted me at every line to say,—

"An armistice? what do *we* want with an armistice? What! after having crushed these Prussians and these Russians at Lutzen, Bautzen, and Wurtschen, ought we not to destroy them utterly?—Would *they*, after beating us, give us an armistice? There it is Joseph, 'tis the Emperor's character, he is too good, —he is too good! It is his only fault.—He did the same thing after Austerlitz, and we had to begin the game again. I tell you he is too good. Ah, if he were not so good, we should be masters of all Europe!"

He looked meanwhile right and left to ask the opinion of the others. But they only made grimaces, and nobody would answer. At last Zimmer got up.

"Let us go, Joseph," he said. "I am not knowing in politics, but I maintain that we ought not to grant an armistice to these rascals: as they are down, we ought to pass over their bodies."

We paid and went out, and Zimmer said again, "I don't know what's the matter with these people; we interrupted them somehow."

"Possibly," I said; "they did not seem to be such good fellows as you described."

"No," said he, "These young fellows, you see, are far below the old students that I have known. *They* passed their life, in a manner, at the brewery; they drank twenty and even thirty pints in the day: even I, Joseph, could not hold my ground against such jolly fellows. Five or six of them, whom they called *seniors*, had grey beards and a venerable air; we sang together *Fanfan-la-Tulipe* and *Le Roi Dagobert*, which are not political songs; but these young men are not like the old ones."

I have often thought since of what we saw that day, and I am sure that those students made part of the *Tugendbund*.

On returning to the hospital, after having a good dinner and a good bottle of white wine each at the *Grappe* tavern, in the Rue Tilly, we learnt that we were to sleep that night—Zimmer and I—at the barracks of Rosenthal. This was a kind of depôt for the wounded of Lützen, when they began to recover. We lived there for the most part as in garrison, having to appear at the roll-call, morning and evening; the rest of the time we were free. Every third day the surgeon came to make his visit, and when you were recovered, you received your note to go and rejoin your corps.

One may imagine the situation of twelve or fifteen hundred poor fellows dressed in grey coats with lead buttons, their heads covered with great shakos shaped like flowerpots, in shoes worn out by marches and counter-marches, pale, haggard, and most of them without a *sou*, in a rich city like Leipzig. We made no great figure among these students, these good citizens, these smiling women; who, in spite of all our glory, regarded us as though we were barefooted beggars. All the fine things my comrade had told me made this state of things but the sadder for me.

It is true that once we had been well received; but our old soldiers had not always behaved as they should to people who had treated them like brothers, and now they shut their doors in our faces. We were reduced to contemplating from morning to night, *Places*, churches, and the fronts of the pork-shops, which are very fine in this part of the world.

We sought for all kinds of distractions; the old ones played at "drogue," the young went to the public-house. We had also, before the barracks, the game of cat and rat, which is played thus: a stake is driven into the ground to which are fastened two cords; the rat is held by one of these cords, the cat by the other; their eyes are bandaged; the cat is armed with a stick and tries to encounter the rat, who pricks up his ears and avoids the cat as much as he can. Thus they turn about on their toes and amuse the company by their cleverness. Zimmer told me, that formerly the honest Germans came in crowds to see this sight, and were heard laughing half a league off whenever the cat touched the rat with the stick. But times were changed; people passed without even turning their heads: in trying to interest them in our favour we only wasted our pains.

During the six weeks Zimmer and I stayed at Rosenthal, we often made the tour of the city, by way of doing something. We went out by the Faubourg of Randstatt and got as far as Lindenau, on the road to Lutzen. There was nothing but bridges, swamps, little wooded islets, as far as the eye could see. There we ate an omelette with bacon at the tavern of *La Carpe*, and washed it down with a bottle of white wine. They no longer gave us anything on credit, as after Jena; I believe, on the contrary, the landlord would have made us pay twice or thrice the price, for the honour of Germany, if my comrade had not known the price of eggs, bacon, and wine as well as any Saxon.

In the evening, when the sun set behind the reeds of the Elster and the Pleisse, we returned to the town, amidst the plaintive croaking of the frogs, which swarm by millions in these marshes.

Sometimes we halted, with folded arms, on the balustrade of a bridge, and gazed upon the old ramparts of Leipzig, its churches, antique buildings, and the castle of Plessenbourg, in the red light of the sunset. The city comes to a point at the junction of the Pleisse and the Partha, just above this spot.* It is fan-shaped; the Faubourg of Halle being at the point, and the seven other faubourgs joining the branches of the fan. We looked also at the thousand arms of the Elster and the Pleisse, interlaced like a net amongst the isles already in the

---

* On the English map the river is the Rötha, not the Partha (or Parde), and at the point here alluded to it joins the *Elster*, not the *Pleisse*, as stated previously.—*Note of Translator.*

shade, while the water shone like gold: we thought it a very fine sight. But if we had known that we should one day have to cross these rivers under the enemies' guns, after having lost the most fearful and the bloodiest of battles, and that whole regiments would disappear in these waters which then delighted our eyes, I think the view would have made us very sorrowful.

At other times we went up the banks of the Pleisse as far as Mark-Kleberg. This was more than a league distant, and everywhere the fields were covered with harvests that were being carried in haste. The people, on their great carts, seemed not to see us; when we made any inquiry they looked as if they did not understand. Zimmer was always ready to go into a passion; but I restrained him, telling him that these rascals only wanted a pretext for falling upon us: and besides, we had orders to spare the population.

"Very well!" said he, "if the war passes this way, let them look out! We have loaded them with benefits: see how they receive us!"

But what showed still more the general ill-will towards us, was what happened the day after the armistice expired. That day, about eleven o'clock, we went to bathe in the Elster; we had just thrown off our clothes, when Zimmerman, seeing a peasant come up on the road to Cormenitz, called out,—

"Hey, comrade! no danger here, is there?"

"No, no; go in boldly," replied the man, "it's a good place."

And Zimmer, having gone in without misgiving, went down fifteen feet. He swam well, but his left arm was still weak, and the force of the current bore him on, without giving him time to cling to the branches of the willows which hung over the water. If by good fortune there had not been a kind of ford further on, allowing him to regain his feet, he would have got between two islands of mud, and never got out again.

The peasant had stopped on the road to see what happened. Anger seized me, and I dressed very quickly, showing him my fist! but he began to laugh, and reached the village in double quick time.

Zimmerman could not contain himself for indignation; he wanted to run to Cormenitz and try to discover this rascal. Unhappily it was impossible: just try to find a man who can hide in one of three or four hundred hovels. And besides, if we should find him, what could we do to him?

We went along the river to a place where there was

footing, and the coolness of the water calmed us. But on re-entering Leipzig, Zimmerman spoke of nothing but revenge.

"All the country is against us," he said; "the citizens give us sour looks, the women turn their backs, the peasants try to drown us, the tavern-keepers refuse us credit—as if we had not conquered them three or four times; and all this comes of our extraordinary kindness: we ought to have declared that we were their masters! We have granted kings and princes to Germany; we have even made dukes, counts, and barons, with the names of their villages; we have showered on them honours, and this is their gratitude!

"Instead of ordering us to respect the population, they should have given us full powers over everybody; then all these vagabonds would have put on another face, and looked pleasantly at us, as in 1806. Force is everything. Conscripts are just made by force; for, if one did not oblige them to go, they would remain at home. Then one makes soldiers out of the conscripts by force, explaining the discipline to them. With soldiers one gains battles by force, and then people give you everything by force; they raise triumphal arches too, and call you heroes, because they are afraid: that's what it is! But the Emperor is too kind; if he wasn't so kind, I should not have risked drowning to-day: at the sight of my uniform only, that peasant would have trembled to tell me a lie."

Re-entering Leipzig, we saw joy painted on the faces of the inhabitants; it did not break out openly, but the citizens meeting in the streets stopped and shook hands, the women went to pay each other visits; a kind of internal satisfaction shone in the eyes even of men and maid-servants and the poorest labourers.

Zimmer observed to me,—

"One would think the Germans were very happy just now; they have such an air of good-humour."

"Yes," I answered, "that's because of the fine weather and the carrying of the harvest."

It was true the weather was very fine, but on reaching the barracks at Rosenthal we perceived our officers at the principal door, talking eagerly. The men on guard listened, and the passers by approached to hear; we were told that the conferences of Prague had been broken off, and that the Austrians had also just declared war against us, which gave us 200,000 men more to deal with.

I have since learned that we were then 300,000

men against 520,000, and that amongst our enemies were two former French generals, Moreau and Bernadotte. Every one can read that in the books; but we did not know it then, and felt sure of winning the day, as we had never yet lost a battle. For the rest, the ill-will shown us did not disquiet us: in time of war the peasants and the citizens in some sort count for nothing; all we have to do with them is to ask them for money and food, which they always give, because they know that, if they don't, they will have it taken from them to the last *sou*.

The day after this great news there was a general visit of inspection, and twelve thousand of the wounded of Lützen who were almost convalescent received orders to rejoin their corps. They went off in companies, with arms and baggage, some following the route of Altenbourg which goes up the river, others that of Wurtzen more to the left. Zimmer was of the number, having himself asked leave to go. I accompanied him till just beyond the gates, and there we embraced with emotion. I remained, my arm being still too weak.

We were now only five or six hundred; amongst them a certain number of fencing-masters, dancing-masters, professors of French elegance—such fine gentlemen as are to be found at the bottom, as it were, of all depôts. I did not care to know them, and my only consolation was to think of Catherine, and sometimes of my old comrades Klipfel and Zébédé, of whom I received no news.

It was a melancholy life: people looked at us with an evil eye; they dared say nothing, knowing that the French army was distant but four days' march, and Blucher and Schwartzenberg much further off. But for that, how they would have taken us by the throat!

One evening the rumour ran that we had just won a great victory at Dresden. There was a general consternation; the inhabitants never came out of their houses. I went to read the Gazette at *La Grappe* tavern, in the Rue Tilly. The French journals all remained on the table; no one opened them but me.

But the following week, at the beginning of September, I saw the same changes in the faces of the people as on the day the Austrians declared against us. I thought that we had had misfortunes; which was true: as I learned afterwards, for the Paris gazettes said nothing about them.

The weather had changed to wet towards the end of

August; rain fell in torrents. I did not go out of barracks any more. Often, seated on my bed, watching from the window the Elster foaming under the deluge, and the trees of the little isles bending beneath the blast, I thought, "Poor soldiers! — poor comrades! what are you doing at this moment? Where are you? Perhaps on the high roads, and in the fields!" And in spite of my dislike to being there, I felt myself less to be pitied than they. But one day the old Surgeon Tardien made his rounds and said to me,—

"Your arm is sound. Come, raise it for me. All right!"

Next day at the roll-call I was made to pass into a hall where were clothes, knapsacks, pouches, and shoes in abundance. I received a musket, two packets of cartridges, and my route for the 6th, at Gauernitz, on the Elbe. This was on the 1st of October. We set out on our march, twelve or fifteen together; the quartermaster, Poitevin, escorted us. On the way, now one, now another changed his direction, to rejoin his own corps; but Poitevin, four infantry soldiers, and I held on our way to the village of Gauernitz.

CHAPTER XVII.

We went, following the high road to Wurtzen, our muskets shouldered, great-coats tucked up, our backs bent under the knapsack, and very down in the mouth, as may be supposed. The rain fell, the wet ran from our shakos into the back of our necks; the wind shook the poplars, whose yellow leaves fluttered around us, announcing the approach of winter: this lasted for hours.

From time to time we fell in with a village, with its sheds, dunghills, and gardens surrounded with palings. The women, standing behind the little dim panes, watched us pass; a dog barked, a man chopping wood at his door turned to follow us with his eyes, and we went on, splashed up to the backbone. At the end of the village we always saw the high road again stretching away out of sight, grey clouds hanging low on the bare fields, and some meagre crows flying off in quick jerks, uttering their melancholy cry.

Nothing so dreary as such a sight; especially when one thinks that winter is approaching, and that we shall have to sleep in the snow. Nobody spoke a word, except the quartermaster Poitevin. He was an old soldier, yellow, wrinkled, with hollow cheeks, moustaches an ell long, and red nose, like all brandy-drinkers. His language was lofty, though mixed with barrack phrases; and when the rain grew heavier, he exclaimed with a burst of eccentric laughter, "Aye, Poitevin: aye, that will teach you to whistle!" This old toper had noticed that I had a few sous in my pocket: he stuck close to me, saying, "Young man, if your knapsack tires you, hand it over to me." But I contented myself with thanking him for his civility.

In spite of my dislike to being with a man who always looked at the public-house signs when we passed through a village, and said, "A glass or so would do one marvellous good just now," I could not help paying for a drink for him now and then; so that he always kept close to me.

We were approaching Wurtzen, and the rain was falling in floods, when the quartermaster exclaimed for the twentieth time, "Aye, Poitevin, such is life; this will teach you to whistle!"

"What the devil is that proverb of yours, quarter-master?" I said. "I should like to know how the rain can teach you to whistle."

"It is not a proverb, young man, it is an idea which occurs to me when I amuse myself." Then after a moment he added: "You must know that in 1806, the epoch at which I was pursuing my studies at Rouen, it occurred to me to hiss a piece at the theatre, with several other young men like myself. Some hissed, others applauded; blows ensued, and the police put us in gaol by dozens. The Emperor, having heard of the affair, said; 'As they are so fond of fighting, let them be incorporated in my armies! They may satisfy their taste there!' And, of course, the thing was done; no one dared breathe a whisper: not even fathers and mothers!"

"You were then a conscript already?" I said.

"No, my father had just bought me a substitute. It was a joke of the Emperor's: one of those jokes which one remembers for a long time. Twenty or thirty of us are dead in misery; some others, instead of filling an honourable place in their own country as doctors, judges, advocates, are become old drunkards. That's what may be called a good farce!"

Then he began to laugh, looking at me from the corner of his eye. I became very thoughtful, and two or three times after, before reaching Gauernitz, I treated this poor fellow to a glass.

Towards five o'clock in the evening, on approaching the village of Risa, we perceived on the left an old mill with its wooden bridge leading to a cross-path. We took this path by way of a cross-cut, and were not more than two hundred paces from the mill, when we heard loud cries. At the same time, two women, one quite old and the other younger, crossed a garden, dragging children after them; they tried to reach a little wood which bordered the road on the ridge in front. Almost immediately we saw several of our soldiers come out of the mill with bags, others coming up out of a cellar in succession with little barrels, which they hastened to place on a cart near the sluice; others brought cows and horses from a stable, whilst an old man, before the door, raised his hands to heaven, and five or six of these rascals surrounded the pale and terrified miller.

That scene—the mill, the dyke, the windows beaten in, the women running away, our soldiers in foraging caps looking like veritable brigands, the old man cursing them, the cows shaking their heads to get free from those who were leading them off while others pricked them behind with their bayonets — I see it all still!"

"Aye," said Poitevin, "they are marauders. We are not far from the army."

"But it is abominable!" I cried. "They are brigands!"

"Yes," said the quartermaster, "'tis contrary to discipline: if the Emperor knew it, they would have been shot like dogs."

We then crossed the little bridge; and as one of the barrels at the back of the cart was being tapped, the soldiers pressed round with a jug, each drinking in turn. This sight revolted the quartermaster, who cried out in a majestic tone,—

"By what authority do you commit this pillage?"

Several turned their heads, and seeing that we were only three, as the others had gone on without stopping, one of them replied,—

"Hey, you old dog, you want your share of the cake: natural enough. But there's no need to turn up your moustaches about that. Come, drink a drop?"

He held out the jug to him; the quartermaster took it, and, looking sideways at me, drank.

"Now, young man," he said, "if you feel a fancy for it! It's a famous wine!"

"No thank you," I said.

Others around us cried, "Now then, come on! come on! it's time!" Others cried, "No, wait—just try again!"

"Come now," said the quartermaster, in the tone of a worthy man. "You know, comrades, you must go peaceably."

"Yes, yes, old gentleman," replied a kind of drum-major, his great cocked hat set awry across his shoulders, and smiling with a scornful expression, his eyes half-closed; "yes, be quiet, we shall pluck the pigeon quite according to rules. We shall be very considerate—very considerate!"

The quartermaster said no more; he was ashamed before me. "What can one do, young man?" he said, as we hastened on to rejoin our comrades; "all's fair in war. One can't let oneself perish!"

I believe he would have stayed, but for the fear of being caught. I was sorrowful, and said to myself: "Such are drunkards! They may have good impulses, but the sight of a jug of wine makes them forget everything."

At last, about ten o'clock in the evening, we discovered bivouac fires on a dark ridge, to the right of the village of Gauernitz, and of an old castle, where also some lights shone; further off in the plain quivered many other fires. The night was clear; the heavy rain had cleared the air. As we approached the bivouac, we heard the call, "Who goes there?"

"France!" replied the quartermaster.

My heart beat violently, thinking that in some minutes I should see my old comrades again, if they were still in this world. Sentinels advanced from a kind of shed, half a musket shot from the village, to come and reconnoitre us. They came close; their officer an old, grey-headed sub, his arm in a sling under his cloak, asked us whence we came, whither we were going, and if we had encountered any parties of Cossacks on the road. The quartermaster answered for us all. The officer then informed us that the Souham division had quitted the environs of Gauernitz in the morning, and told us to follow him, to look at our route papers; this we did in silence, passing round the bivouac fires, where men covered with dry mud slept twenty together: no one stirred.

We arrived at the shed. It was an old brick-work; the roof very large and shaped like an extinguisher rested on pillars six or seven feet from the soil. Behind rose large supplies of wood. It was very comfortable within; the smell of baked earth was diffused around. The furnace-room was littered with soldiers, who slept the sleep of the just with their backs to the wall; the flame illumined them under the gloomy beams. Beside the pillars shone the muskets piled. I seem now to feel that pleasant, penetrating warmth, and to see my comrades, their clothes steaming at a few paces from the furnace, gravely waiting till the officer had done reading their route papers by the red light. An old soldier, bronzed and weather-beaten, alone was up; he was sitting cross-legged, and held between his knees a shoe, which he was mending with an awl and a piece of string.

The officer gave back the route first to me, saying,—

"You will to-morrow rejoin your battalion, two leagues from hence, near Torgau."

Then the old soldier, looking at me, put his hand on the ground to show me that there was room, and I went and sat down by him. I opened my knapsack, and put on other socks and new shoes, which I had received at

Leipzig. This did me good. The old soldier asked me,—

"You are going to join?"

"Yes; the 6th, at Torgau."

"And you come——?"

"From the hospital at Leipzig."

"One can see that," he said; "you're as fat as a capon. You've been fed up on legs of fowls there, whilst we ate over-driven cows."

I looked at my sleeping neighbours. He was right: these poor conscripts were all skin and bone; they were yellow, leaden, and wrinkled like veterans; you would have said they could hold out no longer.

After a moment the old soldier said,—

"You've been wounded?"

"Yes, old friend, at Lützen."

"Four months of hospital!" he said, making a grimace. "What luck! *I* come from Spain. I had flattered myself I should find the *Kaiserlichs* of 1807—sheep, nothing but so many sheep. Ah, well, they've become worse than the guerillas. Everything goes to the bad!"

He spoke thus to himself in an undertone, taking no notice of me, and drew out his two strings like a shoemaker, pressing his lips together. From time to time he tried the shoe, to see if the seam hurt him. Finally, he put the awl in his knapsack, the shoe on his foot, and laid his head on a truss of straw.

I was too fatigued almost to get to sleep; however, at the end of an hour I fell into a deep repose.

Next day I set out again, with the quartermaster Poitevin and three other soldiers of the Souham division. We reached first the road which runs alongside the Elbe. The weather was damp, the wind sweeping the river threw foam up to the pathway. We had been hastening on for an hour, when suddenly the quartermaster called,—

"Attention!"

He had stopped with his nose in the air like a hound on the scent. We all listened without hearing anything, because of the noise of the waves on the shore and the wind in the trees. But Poitevin had a more practised ear than we.

"There's skirmishing down there," he said, pointing to a wood on the right. "The enemy may be in our direction; we must try not to get into the midst of them. The best thing we can do is to shelter under the wood, and pursue our way prudently. We shall see at the other end what goes on. If the Prussians or Russians are there, we shall beat a retreat without their seeing us; if they are French, we shall advance."

Every one agreed that the quartermaster was right, and in my heart I admired the acuteness of this old toper. We turned aside then from the road into the wood, Poitevin in front and we behind, with our muskets ready. We walked slowly, and stopped every hundred paces to listen. The sound of firing came nearer; one after another, the discharges echoed in the ravines. The quartermaster said to us,—

"Those are sharpshooters in observation of a body of cavalry, for the other side does not reply."

It was true. Ten minutes after we perceived amongst the trees a battalion of French infantry preparing to boil their soup in the midst of the heather, and, on the grey plain in the distance, platoons of Cossacks defiling from one village to another. Some sharpshooters were firing on them all along the wood, but they were almost out of reach.

"Here you are at home now, young man," said Poitevin, smiling.

He must have had a good eye to read the number of the regiment at such a distance. I, for my part, looked in vain; I saw nothing but creatures in rags, and so wasted that they all had sharp noses, glittering eyes, and ears standing out from the head because of the falling in of the cheeks. Their great-coats were four times too large for them; one would have thought them mantles, they made such folds on the arms and down the sides. As for the mud, I will say nothing about it.

That day I learnt why the Germans appeared so joyous after our victory of Dresden.

We proceeded towards two or three little tents, round which three or four horses cropped the scanty grass. I saw there Colonel Loraine, detached on the left bank of the Elbe with the third battalion. He was a tall thin man, with dark moustaches, and by no means a gentle aspect. He frowned as he saw us come, and when I presented my route paper, said but one word.

"Go and rejoin your company."

I retired, thinking I should surely recognize some men of the 4th; but since Lützen, companies had been drafted into companies, regiments into regiments, divisions into divisions, so that in reaching the foot of the ridge where the grenadiers were encamped, I recognized nobody. The men, seeing me approach, looked at me askance, as if to say,—

"Is that fellow wanting his share of the broth? Stop a moment! we'll see what *he* brings to the cooking-pot."

I was ashamed to ask the place of my company, when a bony veteran with a long hooked nose like an eagle's beak, and broad shoulders, from which hung his old worn-out great-coat, raising his head and examining me, said in a perfectly unconcerned voice,—

"Why, it's you, Joseph. I thought you had been buried this four months."

Then I recognized poor Zébédé. It seems that my face touched him, for without rising he pressed my hand and called out, "Klipfel, here's Joseph!"

Another soldier, seated beside the neighbouring saucepan, turned his head and said, "Is it you, Joseph? So you're not dead?"

And those were all the compliments I received. Misery had made these men so egotistical that they thought only of their own bodies. Nevertheless, Zébédé retained at bottom a good heart; he told me to sit down beside his cooking-pot, darting at the others one of those glances which caused him to be respected, and offered me his spoon, which he had passed through a button-hole of his great-coat. But I declined, with thanks;

having overnight had the wit to go to the pork-butcher at Risa, and to put into my knapsack a dozen of Bologna sausages, with a good crust of bread and a flask full of brandy. So I opened my knapsack, drew out the string of sausages and gave two to Zébédé: this brought the tears to his eyes. I was thinking of offering some to his comrades, but guessing my intentions, he laid his hand significantly on my arm, and said,—

"What is good to eat is good to keep."

Then he retired from the circle, and we ate and drank *schnaps* together; the others said nothing and looked at us askance. Klipfel, perceiving the odour of garlic, turned his head and called out, "Here, Joseph! come and eat at our cooking-pot. Comrades are always comrades, devil take it!"

"Very good," said Zébédé; "for me, the best comrades are sausages: one finds them just when one wants them." Then he closed my knapsack again, saying, "Keep them, Joseph. I haven't fared so well for a month past. You'll lose nothing by it, never fear."

Half an hour after the roll-call was sounded, the sharpshooters fell back, and Sergeant Pinto, who was amongst them, recognized me. "Well!" he said, "so you've got out of it. I'm very glad; but you've come up at a bad moment. This wretched war!" said he, shaking his head.

The colonel and the commandants mounted on horseback, and we set out on our march again. The Cossacks retired, and we went with our arms sloped. Zébédé marched at my side and related to me what had passed since Lützen; first the great victories of Bautzen and Wurtzen; the forced marches to overtake the enemy, who were retreating; the joy they felt in pushing forward upon Berlin. Then the armistice, during which they were quartered in the little market towns: then the arrival of the veterans of Spain—terrible men habituated to pillage, and who taught the young ones how to live on the peasantry.

Unfortunately, at the end of the armistice, all the world was set against us: people had taken a horror of us; they broke up the bridges in our rear, they gave information to the Prussians, the Russians, and the others of our least movements, and every time we got into a slough, instead of helping us, they tried to thrust us deeper into the mire. The heavy rains had come to finish us. On the day of the battle of Dresden such quantities fell that the Emperor's hat flapped on his shoulders. But when one is victorious, one laughs at such things: one is warm in spite of all, and one can find a change of clothes; what is worst of all is when one is beaten, and has to escape through the mud, with hussars, dragoons, and the rest of them on your track, and one doesn't know, when he catches sight of a distant light in the darkness, whether to go on or perish in the deluge.

Zébédé related all this to me in detail. He told me that, after the victory of Dresden, General Vandamme, who was to have cut off the retreat of the Austrians, had been carried by his extraordinary ardour into a tunnel, as it were, in the direction of Kulm, and that those whom we had beaten the day before, had fallen upon him to right and left, in front and in rear; that he had been taken, with several other generals, and his corps destroyed. Two days after, on the 26th of August, a like accident had happened to our division; as also to the 5th, 6th, and 11th corps, on the heights of Löwenberg. We ought to have crushed the Prussians on this side; but by a false movement of Marshal Macdonald, the enemy had surprised us in the hollow of a ravine, with our guns in the mud, our cavalry in disorder, and our infantry unable to fire any more on account of the driving rain. We had defended ourselves with the bayonet, and the 3rd battalion had, despite constant attacks from the Prussians, reached the river of Katzbach. There Zébédé had received from a grenadier two blows with the butt-end of his musket on the forehead. The current had carried him along while trying to keep Captain Arnould above water, and both would have been lost, had not the captain, dark as the night was, luckily caught hold of a branch of a tree on the other side and got himself out of the water. He told me that all that night, in spite of the blood which flowed from his nose and ears, he had marched to the village of Goldberg, dying of hunger, fatigue and wounds; but that a joiner had had pity on him, and given him bread, onions, and water. He related to me afterwards, that next day the whole division, followed by the other corps, marched in troops across the field of their own accord, without having received orders; because the generals, the marshals, and all the mounted officers had fled as far on as possible for fear of being taken. He assured me that fifty hussars would have picked them all up, one after the other; but that, fortunately, Blucher was not able to cross the river in its flooded state. Thus the division managed to rally at Wolda, where every regiment marched to its quarters in the village by beat of drum; by this means every man got himself clear by marching to the sound of his own drum. The most fortunate thing in this rout was that a little further on, at Bungtlau, the superior officers also rejoined each other, much surprised at finding they still had battalions to command.

This was what my comrade related to me: not to mention the distrust which it behoved us to have of our allies, who, one moment or another, could not fail to fall upon us unprepared. He told us that Marshals Oudinot and Ney had also been beaten, the one at Grossbeeren and the other at Bennewitz. This was very sad; for in these retreats the conscripts perished of exhaustion, sickness, and every kind of suffering. Only the veterans of Spain and Germany, seasoned by hardships, were able to resist these great fatigues.

"In short," said Zébédé, "we have everything against us; the country, the continual rains, and our own generals, who are weary of it all: some are dukes and princes, and are tired of being in the mud instead of reclining in comfortable armchairs; others, like Vandamme, aim at becoming marshals in a hurry, by means of some grand *coup*. We poor devils, who have nothing to gain but to be crippled for the rest of our lives, and are only the sons of the peasants and workmen who fought to abolish the nobility—*we* must perish, that a new nobility may be created!"

I felt then that the poorest, the worst off, are not always the most stupid, and that, by dint of suffering, one arrives at seeing the sad truth. But I said nothing, and besought the Lord to give me strength and courage to support the miseries which all these faults and acts of injustice portended for the future.

We were now between three armies, which sought to combine in order to crush us at a blow; that of the North commanded by Bernadotte, that of Silesia commanded by Blucher, and the army of Bohemia commanded by Schwartzenberg. It was thought by some that we were going to cross the Elbe to fall on the Prussians and the Swedes, by others that we were going to rush upon the Austrians, in the direction of the mountains, as we had done fifty times in Italy and elsewhere. But the enemy had arrived at an understanding of our movements, and when we appeared to be approaching they retired. Above all, they distrusted the Emperor, who could not be at the same time in Bohemia and Silesia;

and this caused abominable marching and counter-marching.

All that the soldiers asked was to fight; for what with marching and sleeping in the mud, living on half-rations and being devoured by vermin, they had taken a disgust of life. Every one thought, "If it would but finish one way or another! It is too much —it can't last."

For myself, in a few days I was weary of such an existence; I felt my ribs starting out from my skin, and I wasted away visibly.

Every evening a sentry had to be posted, on account of a rascal named Thielmann, who raised the peasantry against us; he followed us like our shadow, he watched us from village to village, on the heights, on the roads, in the hollows of the valleys. His army was composed of all those who hated us: and he had always followers enough.

It was about this time that the Bavarians, the Badeners, and the Wurtembergers declared against us; so that we had all Europe upon us.

At last we had the consolation of seeing that the army gathered itself together as for a great battle; instead of encountering the Cossacks of Platow and the partisans of Thielmann in the environs of the villages, we found hussars, chasseurs, Spanish dragoons, artillery, pontoon trains on the march. The rain fell in torrents, and those who had no longer strength to drag themselves on, sat down in the mud at the foot of a tree, and abandoned themselves to their cruel fate.

On the 11th October we bivouacked near the village of Lousig; the 12th, near Grafenheinichen; the 13th, we passed the Mulda, and saw defile on the bridge the old guard with La Tour Maubourg. The passage of the Emperor was announced, but we departed with the Dombrowski division and Souham's corps.

At moments when the rain ceased to fall, and a ray of the autumn sun gleamed between the clouds, the whole army might be seen on the march; the cavalry and the infantry advancing from all directions on Leipzig. On the other side of the Mulda glittered the bayonets of the Prussians; but the Austrians and Russians could not yet be espied: they were coming no doubt from elsewhere.

On the 14th, our battalion was once more detached, to make a *reconnaissance* in the town of Aachen; the enemy was there and received us with volleys of artillery.

We remained all the night outside, unable to light a single fire, on account of the rain. Next day we left the place, to rejoin our division by forced marches. I don't know why every one was saying, "The battle is coming! the battle is coming!"

Sergeant Pinto asserted that he felt the Emperor in the air. I, for my part, felt nothing of the sort; but I saw that we were marching on Leipzig, and I thought, "If we have a battle, may I only escape such a hit as I got at Lützen, and may I once more see Catherine!"

The following night the weather was rather better; myriads of stars illumined the skies, and we kept going forward. Next day about ten o'clock, near a little village whose name I can't remember, the order "Halt," was given, to allow us breathing time; then we all of us heard something like a loud humming in the air. The colonel, still on horseback, listened. Sergeant Pinto said,—"The battle is begun!"

At almost the same moment, the colonel, waving his sword, shouted "Forward!"

Then we began to run; knapsacks, pouches, guns, mud, were dancing about us: we took heed of nothing. Half-an-hour afterwards, we descried at some thousand paces before the battalion, a column which seemed to have no ending; waggons, cannon, infantry, cavalry; behind us, on the Duben road, more were coming, and all at a gallop! Even across country, whole regiments came up at a run.

At the very end of the road, we could see the steeples of Saint Nicholas and St. Thomas of Leipzig against the sky, while right and left, on the two sides of the city, rose great clouds of smoke, or lightnings flashed. The rumbling sound kept increasing; we were still more than a mile from the city when we were forced to speak loud in order to be heard, and we looked at each other with pale faces, as though to say,—" This is a battle indeed!"

Sergeant Pinto exclaimed,—" 'Tis hotter than at Eylau!" He did not laugh; nor Zébédé, nor I, nor the others; but we pressed on all the same, and the officers incessantly repeated, " Forward! forward!" That is how men lose their heads! certainly the love of our country animated us, but the fighting frenzy was more ardent still.

About eleven o'clock, we descried the battle-field, within a league from Leipzig. We also saw the steeples of the city covered with people, and the old ramparts, where I had so often walked thinking of Catherine.

In front of us, twelve or fifteen hundred yards off, were ranged two regiments of red lancers, and a little to the left, two or three regiments of mounted *chasseurs*, in the meadows of the Partha. It was between these regiments that the convoys which came from Duben defiled. Further off, skirting a little ridge, were ranged in *échelon*, the divisions of Ricard, Dombrowski, Souham, and several others, with their backs turned to the city. Ammunition waggons and cannon stood with the horses harnessed to them—gunners and artillerymen were on horseback—all were ready to move. Finally, quite behind, on the hill, around one of those old farms with flat-roofs and large penthouses such as one sees in this country, glittered the uniforms of the staff.

This was the army of reserve, commanded by Marshal Ney; his left wing communicated with Marmont, posted on the road to Halle, his right wing with the great army, commanded by the Emperor in person. Thus our troops formed, so to speak, a great circle round Leipzig; and our enemies, coming from all sides at once, sought to join hands with each other, to make a still wider circle around us, and shut us up in the city as in a trap.

Meanwhile, three terrible battles were going on at once; one against the Austrians and Russians, at Wachau; another against the Prussians, at Möckern, on the Halle road; and the third on the road to Lützen, to defend the bridge of Lindenau, attacked by General Giulay.

All this I did not know till afterwards: but each one must relate what he saw himself; in this manner the world will know the truth.

CHAPTER XVIII.

The battalion began to descend the hill in front of Leipzig, to join our division, when we saw a staff-officer cross the great meadow below, and come full gallop in our direction. In two minutes he was with us; Colonel Loraine went to meet him; they exchanged some words, then the officer turned back again. Hundreds of other officers went thus about the plain bearing orders.

"Right wheel!" cried the colonel, and we took the direction of a wood in our rear, which skirts the Duben road for about half-a-league: it was a forest of beeches, but there were also birches and oaks. Once on the skirts of the wood, we were ordered to renew our priming, and the battalion was deployed as skirmishers. We were drawn up at twenty-five paces from each other, and we advanced, keeping our eyes wide open, as may be imagined. Sergeant Pinto said every minute—

"Put yourselves under cover!"

But he had no need to warn us so much; every one pricked up his ears, and hastened to shelter behind a great tree, in order to look out in safety before going further. To think what peaceable men may be exposed to in this life!

We had been marching thus for ten minutes, and, as we saw nothing, confidence began to return to us, when a musket-shot rang—then one, then two, three, six, from all sides, all along our line; and at the same time I saw my comrade on the left fall, whilst trying to support himself against a tree. This roused me. I glanced to the other side, and what should I see, fifty or sixty paces off, but an old Prussian soldier, with his little cap with its chain, his elbow crooked, and his great reddish moustaches drooping over the hammer of his rifle, aiming at me with half-closed eyes. I stooped down as quick as thought. That very moment I heard the report, and something cracked over my head: the brush, the comb, and the handkerchief in my shako —the rascal's bullet had shattered them all. I felt cold all over.

"Well! you've had a narrow escape!" cried out the sergeant, beginning to run; and I, not wishing to remain alone in such a place, followed him very quickly.

Lieutenant Bretonville, his sabre under his arm, repeated "Forward! forward!" Further on, upon the right, the firing continued. But we had now reached the edge of our glade, where were five or six great fallen trunks of oaks, a small pool full of long grass, and not a single tree to cover us. Nevertheless, several were advancing boldly, when Sergeant Pinto cried, "Halt!—the Prussians are sure to be in ambush in the neighbourhood; let's look about us."

Scarcely had he said it than a dozen bullets whistled through the branches, and the air resounded with the reports; at the same time a body of Prussians were seen scampering deeper into the thicket.

"There, they're off; come on!" said Pinto.

"But the shot in my shako had put me on the alert, so I managed to peep between the trees; and, as the sergeant was about to traverse the clearing, I held him back by the arm, pointing out to him the tip of a rifle which projected beyond a large bush, on the other side of the pool, a hundred paces before us. Our comrades, coming up, saw it too, which made the sergeant say in a low voice, "You, Bertha, stay here! keep him in view!—we'll turn the position!"

Immediately they dispersed to right and left; and I, musket on shoulder, behind my tree, listened like a hunter for his prey. In two or three minutes, the Prussian, hearing nothing more, quietly arose. He was quite young, with a small light moustache, and a tall, slender figure, in a close-fitting uniform: I could have knocked him over with ease; but the idea of killing this man thus exposed, had such an effect on me that I trembled. Suddenly he perceived me and sprung to one side. Then I discharged my piece, and breathed again freely when I saw him bounding through the copse like a deer.

At the same time, five or six musket-shots were discharged right and left; Sergeant Pinto, Zébédé, Klipfel, and others, passed like an arrow, and a hundred paces further, we found the young Prussian on the ground, his mouth filled with blood: he looked at us all scared, lifting his arm as if to parry the bayonet thrusts. The sergeant said to him gleefully, "Don't be afraid! *You've* got your business settled!"

Nobody cared to finish the work. Klipfel took a

handsome pipe which stuck out of his pocket behind, saying, "I've been wanting a pipe for a long time, and here's one!"

"Fusilier Klipfel," exclaimed Pinto, "please to put back that pipe! Leave it to the Cossacks to plunder the wounded! The French soldier knows nothing but honour!"

Klipfel threw away the pipe, and finally we left the spot without turning our heads. We reached the end of this thicket, which ended three-quarters of the way up the ridge; but tufted brushwood extended to within two hundred paces of the top, and the Prussians whom we had pursued were hidden inside: we saw them start up on every side to fire at us, and then crouch down again immediately.

We could easily have remained there quietly, having orders to occupy the wood, and the brushwood not troubling us; behind the trees where we were, the volleys of the Prussians would have done us no harm. We heard a terrible battle on the other side of the ridge, the discharges of cannon followed in quick succession, and sometimes thundered in volleys like a storm; which was a reason the more for staying where we were. But our officers, assembling together, decided that the brushwood was part of the forest, and that we must chase the Prussians up to the ridge. This caused the loss of many of our people in this place.

Accordingly we received orders to pursue the hostile skirmishers, and as they fired the more the nearer we approached and then hid themselves, everybody began running upon them to prevent them from loading again. Our officers ran too, full of ardour. We thought that on the top of the hill the brushwood would cease, and that then we should shoot down the Prussians by dozens; but at the moment that we reached the top all out of breath, old Pinto cried out, "The hussars!"

I raised my head, and saw caps ascending and growing more numerous behind this species of saddle-back: they came upon us like the wind. Scarcely had I seen this than, without reflecting, I turned and began to re-descend, springing fifteen feet at a time, in spite of the fatigue, in spite of my knapsack and everything: I saw before me Sergeant Pinto, Zébédé, and the others, who hurried on, leaping at full stretch of their legs. Behind, the hussars *en masse* made such a noise that one felt one's flesh creep; the officers gave orders in German, the horses snorted, the sabre-scabbards rung against their wearers' stirrups, and the earth shook!

I had taken the shortest way to reach the wood, and almost thought I was there, when, close to the edge, I fell in with one of those deep ditches where the peasants dig for stiff clay to build with: it was more than twenty feet wide and forty or fifty long. The rain, which had been falling some days, made the edges very slippery; but when I heard the horses snorting more and more, the hair stood upright on my head, and, heedless of everything, I made a dash and fell into this hole, on my back, my cartridge-pouch and great-coat turned up over my head. Another fusilier of my company was there, just picking himself up, he also having tried to jump. At the same moment, two hussars, dashing at full speed along this muddy slope, on their horses' croups, the first of them with his face all red, dealt a blow with his sabre on the ear of my poor comrade, swearing like a madman. As he raised his arm to finish him, I plunged my bayonet with all my might into his side; but at the same time the other hussar gave me a blow on the shoulder, which, but for the epaulette, would have cleft me in two: he was going to run me through, if by good luck a musket-shot from above had not blown his brains out. I looked and saw one of my comrades plunged in the stiff clay up to the knee. He had heard the neighings of the horses and the swearing of the hussars, and had advanced to the brink of the hole to see what was happening.

"Well, comrade!" he said laughing, "just in time!" I had no power to answer him: I trembled like a leaf. He took off his bayonet, and held out to me the end of his gun to help me to get out again. Then I took this soldier's hand and said,—

"You have saved my life! . . . . What is your name?"

He told me that his name was Jean Pierre Vincent. I have often thought since that if I should meet this man, I should be glad to do him a service; but two days after, the second battle of Leipzig took place, then the retreat on Hanau, and I have never seen him again.

Sergeant Pinto and Zébédé came an instant later. Zébédé said to me, "We have been in luck again, we two, Joseph; we are the last Phalsbourgians of the battalion now . . . . Klipfel has just been cut to pieces by the hussars!"

"You saw it?" I said, turning quite pale.

"Yes, he received more than twenty sabre cuts. He cried out, 'Zébédé! Zébédé!'"

An instant after, he added, "For all that, it's terrible to hear an old comrade, whom one has known from one's childhood, call for help, without being able to give it! But they were too many!—they surrounded him!"

This saddened us, and the thought of our country recurred to us once more. I pictured to myself the grandmother Klipfel, when she heard the news, and this thought made me think also of Catherine!

After the charge of the hussars till the night, the battalion remained in the same position, firing at the Prussians. We prevented them from occupying the wood; but they prevented us from ascending the ridge. The next day we knew why. This ridge commands the whole course of the Partha, and the great cannonade that we heard came from the Dombrowski division, who were attacking the left wing of the Prussian army, and who wanted to relieve General Marmont at Mochern. There, twenty thousand Frenchmen posted on a ravine, held Blucher's eighty thousand men in check; and in the direction of Wachau, a hundred and fifteen thousand French gave battle to two hundred thousand Austrians and Russians. More than fifteen hundred pieces of cannon were volleying. Our poor little *fusillade* on the ridge of

Wetterich was like the humming of a bee in the midst of the storm. And sometimes even we ceased firing, on both sides, to listen. It seemed to me something fearful, and, so to speak, supernatural: the air was full of smoke and the earth trembled under our feet. Old soldiers like Pinto said they had never heard anything like it.

Towards six o'clock a staff-officer came upon our left, bringing an order from Colonel Loraine, and almost inmediately the retreat was sounded. The battalion had lost sixty men in the charge of the Prussian hussars and the *fusillade*. It was night when we issued from the forest; and on the banks of the Partha, among powder chests, convoys of all sorts, bodies of men in retreat, detachments, and waggons bearing the wounded defiling over two bridges, we had to wait more than two hours for our turn to come. The sky was dark, the cannonading growled still from time to time; but the three battles were over. We heard it said that we had beaten the Austrians and Russians at Wachau, on the other side of Leipzic; but those who returned from Möckern were gloomy: nobody cried "Vive l'Empereur!" as after a victory.

Once on the other side, the battalion descended the Partha for a good half league, to the village of

Schönfeld. The night was damp; we marched with a heavy step, musket on shoulder, our eyes shut from drowsiness, and our heads bent. Behind us, the long train of guns, ammunition-carts, baggage and troops, retreating from Möckern, prolonged their heavy roll; and at intervals the shouts of the artillerymen and the drivers forcing their way, rose above the tumult. But these noises gradually died away, and at length we arrived near a cemetery, where the ranks were broken and the muskets piled.

Then at last I raised my head, and recognized Schönfeld by the moonlight. How often had I gone to eat good fritters there, and drink white wine with Zimmer at the little tavern of the *Gerbe d'Or*, under the vine-trellis of father Winter, when the sun warmed the air, and the verdure shone around us! . . . . Those times were past!

Sentinels were posted: some men entered the village to look for wood and victuals. I seated myself against the cemetery wall and fell asleep. Towards three o'clock I was waked up.

"Joseph," said Zébédé to me, "come and warm yourself; if you stay there, you run a risk of taking a fever."

I rose as if tipsy, with fatigue and suffering. A small fine rain drizzled in the air. My comrade dragged me near the fire, which smoked under the rain. This fire was only for look: it gave no warmth; but Zébédé having made me drink a drop of brandy, I felt a little less cold. I looked at the bivouac fires, which blazed on the other side of the Partha.

"The Prussians are getting up the steam," said Zébédé, "they are now in our wood."

"Yes," I replied, "and poor Klipfel is down there too: *he* feels the cold no longer!"

My teeth chattered. These words made us sad. Some instants after, Zébédé asked me, "Don't you remember, Joseph, the black ribbon which he had in his hat the day of the conscription; and how he said, 'We are all condemned to death, like those in Russia. I will have a black ribbon: we must wear mourning for ourselves.' And his little brother said, 'No, Jacob, I don't want you to,' and cried. But Klipfel put it on nevertheless: he had seen the hussars in a dream."

As Zébédé spoke, I saw again that rascal Pinacle on the *Place* of the Hôtel de Ville, who called out to me, waving a black ribbon over his head, "Ha, cripple, you must have a fine ribbon, too: the winner's ribbon?

Come on!" This idea, with the terrible cold, which pierced to my very marrow, made me shiver, and I thought, "I shall never return. All is over."

About four o'clock, as morning began to brighten the sky, some carts came up with provisions; bread was dealt out to us, and we received also meat and brandy. The rain had ceased. We cooked our soup here; but nothing could warm me: I had caught the fever. I was not the only one in the battalion in this state; three-fourths of them suffered and wasted away thus. For a month past, those who could no longer march had been lying down on the ground, weeping and calling to their mothers like little children. It was a scene to pierce one's heart. Hunger, forced marches, rain, and the grief of knowing that one would never see one's country again, caused this malady. Happily, parents don't see their children dying along the route: it would be too terrible if they did. Many would think that there was no mercy, either in heaven or on earth.

Gradually, as the daylight grew, we descried, on the other side of the river and of a great ravine filled with willows and aspens, burned villages, heaps of dead, powder chests and guns overturned, and the land ravaged as far as one could see, on the Halle, Lindenthal, and Dolitzsch roads: it was worse than at Lützen. We saw, too, the Prussians deploying in this direction, and advancing by thousands on the battle-field. They were going to join the Austrians and Russians, and close in a circle round us: no one now could hinder them; especially as Bernadotte and the Russian general Beningsen, who had remained behind, now came up with 120,000 fresh troops. Thus our army, after having fought three battles in one day and being reduced to 130,000 combatants, was to be caught in a circle of 300,000 bayonets, without reckoning 50,000 horses and 1200 guns!

From Schönfeld, the battalion was again set marching to rejoin the division at Kohlgarten. All the way one saw convoys of wounded passing slowly on; all the country carts had been put in requisition for this service, and among them marched hundreds more of these poor fellows, their arms in slings, or their faces bandaged, pale, dejected, half dead. None but those wholly unable to drag themselves along got on the cart, though all were striving to reach a hospital.

We had no end of trouble in getting past these obstacles, when all of a sudden, on our approaching Kohlgarten, about twenty hussars, with pistols in hand, coming at full speed, forced the crowd back right and left into the fields. They shouted with loud voices,—"The Emperor! the Emperor!"

Immediately the battalion drew aside, presenting arms along the footway, and some seconds after, the mounted grenadiers of the guard—veritable giants, with their great boots and immense fur caps which came down to their shoulders—passed at a gallop, their sabre-hilts resting firmly upon their hips. Every one said with complacency to himself, "These men are with us: these stout bold fellows!"

Scarcely had they defiled past when the staff appeared. Picture to yourselves from one hundred and fifty to two hundred generals, marshals, superior officers and orderlies, mounted on horses swift as deer, and so covered with gold embroidery and decorations that one scarcely saw the colour of their uniforms; some were tall and thin, with a haughty air, others short and thick, with red faces; others, younger, sat upright on their horses like statues, with shining eyes and great eagle-noses: it was something at once magnificent and terrible!

But what struck me most, in the midst of all these captains who had made Europe tremble for twenty years, was Napoleon, with his old hat and grey surtout: I see him now pass before my eyes, his large chin compressed and his neck sunk in his shoulders. All present cried, "*Vive l'Empereur!*" But he seemed to hear nothing: he took no more heed of us than he did of the small fine drizzling rain; but gazed with knitted brow at the Prussian army, extending along the Partha to unite with the Austrians.

The battalion had been in march again for a quarter of an hour, when Zébédé said to me, "Did you see him, Joseph?"

"Yes," I answered, "I saw him well; and I shall remember it all my life."

"It's droll," said my comrade: "one would say he wasn't pleased. . . . At Wartschen, the day after the battle, he seemed so joyous at hearing us shout, '*Vive l'Empereur;*' and the generals, too, had a smile on their faces! Now, they all look in a devil of a temper. The captain said though, this morning, that we had won the battle on the other side of Leipzig."

Many others thought the same thing without saying anything; and uneasiness took possession of us.

We found the regiment bivouacking at two musket-ranges from Kohlgarten. The battalion took up a position to the right of the road, on a hill. In all directions we saw the smoke from the innumerable fires of the various armies rise up to the sky. There was still a drizzling rain, and the men seated on their knapsacks opposite the little fires, with folded arms, seemed all to be in a reverie: the officers were grouped together. The same remarks were everywhere heard, that such a war had never been seen; that it was a war of extermination; that the enemy did not mind being beaten, and only wanted to make a slaughter among us, well knowing that when all was over he would have four or five thousand more men than we, and would remain master of the field.

It was also remarked that though the Emperor had been victorious at Wachau against the Austrians and Russians, it had been to no purpose, since they did not retreat, but waited for large bodies of reinforcements. It was known that in the direction of Möckern we had been beaten, in spite of Marmont's admirable defence: the enemy had overwhelmed us with numbers. We had gained but one real advantage this day: that namely, of having kept open our line of retreat upon Erfürt; for Giulay had been unable to seize the bridges of the Elster and the Pleisse. The whole army, from the common soldier to the marshal, thought that what we had to do was to retreat as soon as possible, and that we were in a very bad position. Unhappily the Emperor thought otherwise, and we had to stay where we were.

This whole day, the 17th, we remained in position without firing a single shot. Some talked of the arrival of General Regnier, with sixteen thousand Saxons; but the defection of the Bavarians had taught us how little confidence was to be placed in our allies.

Towards evening came the announcement that the army of the North began to be visible on the plateau of Breitenfeld; it was an addition of sixty thousand men to the enemy. I seem still to hear the curses that were poured forth against Bernadotte—the cries of indignation from all those who had known him a simple officer in the time of the Republic, and who said,—"He owes everything to us: we made him king with our own blood, and now he is coming to give us the *coup de grâce!*"

At night a general movement to the rear took place; our army closed more and more around Leipzig, when everything remained quiet again. But that did not hinder reflection; on the contrary, each man thought to himself—"What is going to happen to-morrow? shall I indeed, at this same hour, see the moon rise amongst the clouds, as I see her now? Will the stars shine for me once more?"

And when, through the gloom of night, we looked at the great circle of fire which surrounded us to an extent of nearly six leagues, we cried to ourselves,—

"Now the whole universe is against us! All nations desire our extermination—they have had enough of our glory!"

And then we thought how, at all events, we had the honour of being Frenchmen, and that we must conquer or die.

CHAPTER XIX.

Day broke upon us in the midst of these thoughts. Nothing was yet stirring, and Zébédé said to me, "Suppose the enemy had not the courage to attack us! what good luck it would be."

The officers, too, were talking amongst themselves about an armistice. But all of a sudden, about nine o'clock, our scouts came galloping back, crying out that the whole line of the enemy was in motion, and almost immediately after, the cannon thundered on our right, along the Elster. We were already under arms, and we marched across the field in the direction of the Partha, to return to Schönfeld. It was there the battle began. On the hills, in front of the river, two or three divisions were waiting for the enemy, their batteries posted between them, and the cavalry on their flanks; further off, just over the points of their bayonets, we saw the

Prussians, Swedes, and Russians advancing in deep masses, from all sides: there seemed no end of them.

Twenty minutes after, we came up in line, and descried before us five or six thousand Prussians crossing the river, and all crying out together,—"*Vaterland! Vaterland!*" The tumult was immense; much like that made by those clouds of crows we see flocking together to go northwards.

At the same moment the musket firing began from one bank to the other, the cannon opened their thunder, and the ravine through which flowed the Partha, was filled with smoke. The Prussians were already upon us, before we could well see them, with their fierce eyes, their projecting mouths, and their wild-beast-like look. Then we all sent up to heaven but one shout,—"*Vive l'Empereur!*" and rushed upon them. The *mêlée* became frightful. In a moment our bayonets crossed each other by thousands! We pressed on, we recoiled, we dealt each other deadly blows with the butt-ends of muskets; all ranks were confounded together: those who fell were marched over. The cannon thundered, and the smoke which crept over the gloomy water between the hills, the whistling of the balls, and the blazing of the *fusillade*, made the ravine resemble an oven, where the men were engulfed like logs for the burning.

For our parts, it was despair which impelled us, and mad desire to avenge ourselves before we died; with the Prussians, it was the pride of saying,—"We are going to conquer Napoleon this time!" These Prussians are the proudest of men; their victories of Gross-Beeren and the Katzbach almost maddened them! But many of them were left in the river—ay many! Three times they crossed the water and rushed upon us *en masse.* We were inevitably forced back on account of their great number, and what cries they raised then! One would have said they wished to eat us. They are a bad set of people. Their officers waving their swords between the close ranks of bayonets, repeated a hundred times "Forwards! forwards!" and all advanced like a wall, with great courage: it can't be denied. Our guns swept them down, yet they still advanced; but at the top of the hill we regained fresh spirit and drove them into the river. We should have massacred them all, but for one of their batteries before Möckern, which took us in flank, and prevented us from pursuing them further.

This lasted till two o'clock. Half of our officers

were disabled: Commandant Gémeau was wounded, Colonel Loraine killed. All along the river one saw nothing but heaps of dead and wounded, who dragged themselves along to get out of the crush; some, furious, raised themselves to their knees, to give one more bayonet thrust or fire a last shot. Never was anything seen like it. In the river floated the dead; some showing their faces, some their backs, others their feet: they followed each other like floats of timber, and nobody took any notice of it.

This great carnage took place all along the Partha, from Schönfeld to Grossdorf. The Swedes and Prussians finished by re-ascending the river to turn us higher up, and large bodies of Russians came to replace these Prussians, who were not sorry to go on some other business. The Russians, formed in two columns, descended to the ravine with fixed bayonets, in admirable order, and twice assaulted us with great bravery, but without raising savage cries like the Prussians; their cavalry tried to carry the old bridges above Schönfeld. The cannonade grew heavier and heavier; in all directions where the eye could reach across the smoke, nothing was to be seen but enemies closing up. When we had repulsed one of their columns, there always came up another with fresh troops: we always had to begin again.

Between two or three o'clock we learned that the Swedes and the Prussian cavalry had passed the river above Grossdorf, and taken us in the rear: they liked that much better than attacking us in front. Marshal Ney immediately changed front, the right wing being sent to the rear. Our division remained resting on Schönfeld, but all the others retired from the Partha, to be drawn up in the plain, and the whole army formed but one line round Leipzic.

The Russians behind the Möckern road prepared their third attack about three o'clock, and our officers made new dispositions to receive them; when a kind of shiver passed from one end of the army to the other: for in a few minutes all knew that the 16,000 Saxons and the Würtemberg cavalry in the centre of our line had just gone over to the enemy, and that even before getting beyond the range of fire, they had had the infamy to turn the forty pieces of cannon which they had taken with them, against their former brothers-in-arms of the Durutt division. But this treason, instead of depressing us, so greatly increased our fury, that if we had had our way, we should have crossed the river to exterminate them.

These Saxons say that they were defending their

country; but it is false. They had only to quit us on the Duben road: what was there to prevent them? They could have done like the Bavarians, and declared themselves before the battle; they might have remained neuter, they might have refused to serve; but they betrayed us, because the luck was turning against us. If they had seen that we were going to win, they would have always been our good friends, in order to get *their* share of the gains; as after Jena and Friedland. That was what every one thought; and that is why these Saxons will be held traitors from age to age. Not only did they abandon their friends in misfortune, but they assassinated them, to secure themselves a good welcome from others. God is just. Their new allies had such contempt for them, that they shared among themselves the half of their country after the battle. The French have laughed at the gratitude of the Prussians, Austrians, and Russians.

From that moment till the evening it was no more a common war that was waged—it was a war of vengeance. We were doomed to be crushed by numbers; but the allies had to pay dear for their victory.

At nightfall, whilst 2,000 pieces of cannon were thundering together, we sustained our seventh attack at Schönfeld: on one side the Russians and on the other the Prussians, pressed upon us in this large village. We held every house, every alley; the walls fell under the balls, the roofs crumbled: there was no more shouting as at the commencement; we turned cold and pale for very rage. The officers had caught up muskets, and buckled on cartridge pouches, tearing the cartridges like any soldier. After the houses, we defended the gardens and the cemetery, where I had slept the night before. There were then more dead above than below ground. Those who fell made no complaint; those who remained, clustered behind a wall, a heap of ruins, or a tomb: every inch of ground cost a life.

It was night when Marshal Ney brought us reinforcements—I know not whence; what remained of the Ricard division and the second of Souham. All the scattered fragments of our regiments were collected, and we forced back the Russians to the other side of the old bridge, which had been riddled with grape-shot till there were no railings left. Six twelve-pounders were placed on this bridge, and up to seven o'clock cannonading went on upon this spot. The remains of the battalion and of some others behind served the guns; and I remember that their fire passed under the bridge like lightning-flashes, and that we saw the slaughtered horses and men engulfed pell-mell under the gloomy arches. It lasted only a second: but these were terrible sights!

At half-past seven, as large bodies of artillery advanced upon our right, and we saw them surging round two great squares which were retiring step by step, we received at last the order to retreat. There remained no more than two or three thousand men at Schönfeld, with six pieces. We returned to Kohlgarten without being pursued, and we went to bivouac round Rendnitz. Zébédé was still living. As we marched beside each other in silence for twenty minutes listening to the cannonade, which continued in spite of the night in the Elster direction, all at once he said—

"How is it we are still here, Joseph, when so many thousand others fell at our side? Surely we cannot now be killed!"

I made no answer. "What a battle!" he continued; "was there ever such fighting before? 'Tis impossible."

He was right: it was a battle of giants. From ten o'clock in the morning till seven in the evening we had held our ground against 360,000 men, without recoiling a foot; and we meanwhile were but 130,000! Never was the like seen. God forbid that I should speak ill of the Germans: they combated for the independence of their country; but I think they are wrong in celebrating every year the anniversary of the battle of Leipzig: when they were three to one, what is there to boast of?

Approaching Rendnitz, we marched over heaps of corpses. At every step we fell in with dismounted cannons, overturned waggons, trees cut to pieces by grape-shot. It was there that a division of the young guard and mounted grenadiers, led by Napoleon himself, had checked the Swedes, who were advancing in the gap formed by the treachery of the Saxons. Two or three old hovels which were just being burnt down in front of the village, lighted up this scene. The mounted grenadiers were still at Rendnitz; but a crowd of other dispersed troops went and came in the main street. Rations not having been given out, every one was seeking for something to eat and drink.

As we were defiling before a large posthouse, we saw behind the wall of a courtyard two *cantinières*, who were pouring out drink from the top of their carts.

There were chasseurs, cuirassiers, lancers, hussars, infantry of the line, and the guard, all pell-mell, with tattered shakos and helmets battered in, without plumes and riddled with shots—and all these men seemed famished.

Two or three dragoons, standing on the little wall, near a pot filled with peas boiling, their arms folded under their long white cloaks, were covered with blood like butchers. Zébédé immediately, without saying anything, nudged me with his elbow, and we entered the court, whilst the others pursued their way. It took us a quarter-of-an-hour to get to the cart. I held up a six-franc piece; the *cantinière*, kneeling beside her barrel, held out to me a large glass of brandy with a piece of white bread, taking my money. I drank, and then passed the glass to Zébédé, who emptied it. We had then much trouble in getting out of the crowd; men looked round with a gloomy air, and made room for themselves with shoulders and elbows. One might well say there—seeing those hard faces, those hollow eyes, those terrible aspects of men who had passed through a thousand deaths, and would recommence to-morrow—"Each one for himself! God for all!"

Going up the village-street again, Zébédé said, "Have you bread?"—"Yes." I broke it in two and gave him half: we ate as we hastened on. There was still a sound of firing in the distance. In twenty minutes we had caught up the rest of the column, and we recognized the battalion by the adjutant-major Captain Vidal, who was walking near. We re-entered the ranks without any one having remarked our absence. The nearer we approached the city, the more detachments of cannons and baggage did one meet hastening to Leipzig.

Towards ten o'clock we passed through the faubourg of Rendnitz. The general of brigade Fournier took the command of us, and gave us the order to slope to the left. At midnight we reached the long promenades which skirt the Pleisse; we halted under the old lime-trees, now stripped bare, and arms were piled. A long row of fires quivered in the mist as far as the faubourg of Randstadt, and when the flame mounted, it threw a light on groups of Polish lancers, rows of horses, guns and waggons, and, at long intervals, on the sentinels, motionless in the dusk like shadows. Loud noises arose in the city, ever increasing and mingling with the dull roll of our convoys on the bridge of Lindenau. It was the beginning of the retreat. Then each one of us laid his knapsack at the foot of a tree, and stretched himself upon it, his arm folded under his ear. A quarter-of-an-hour afterwards everybody was asleep.

CHAPTER XX.

WHAT passed during the night I know not: baggage, wounded, and prisoners continued doubtless to defile over the bridge; but at daybreak a fearful report awoke us:—not a man remained recumbent, as we took the sound for an assault, when two officers of hussars arrived, calling out that a powder-waggon had just exploded by chance in the great avenue of Randstadt, by the water's edge. The smoke, of a dark red colour, was whirling in the air, as it dispersed; the earth and the old houses trembled.

Quiet was soon restored, and some lay down again to try and fall asleep once more; but day was breaking. Glancing towards the grey light on the river, we saw our troops already drawn up as far as the eye could reach, on the five bridges which lie so close to each other as to make as it were but one over the Elster and the Pleisse. The sight of this bridge, on which so many thousands of men were to defile, made one very melancholy. The passage would take a good deal of time, and the idea occurred to everybody that it would have been much better to have thrown other bridges across the two rivers; since from one moment to another the enemy might attack us, and then retreat would become very difficult. But the Emperor had forgotten to give orders, and no one dared do anything without: not a marshal of France would have dared take upon him to say that two bridges were better than one. And this was what the terrible discipline of Napoleon had reduced all these old captains to; they obeyed like machines, and troubled themselves about nothing further, for fear of displeasing their master!

All of a sudden, seeing this never-ending bridge, I thought, "If only they will let us now defile past! for, please God, we have had enough of battles and carnage! Once upon the other side, we shall be on the good old road to France; I shall perhaps see Catherine again, Aunt Grédel, and Father Goulden!" I melted at these thoughts; I gazed with envy on those thousands of mounted artillerymen and soldiers accompanying the guns, who were swarming away like ants, and the huge fur-caps of the Old Guard, motionless on the other side of the river, on the hill of Lindenau, with fixed bayonets. Zébédé, who had the same thought, said to me, "Ah, Joseph! if we were but in their place!"

Again, about seven o'clock, when we saw three waggons coming up to distribute cartridges and bread, I had very bitter feelings. It was clear now that we should be in the rear-guard, and, spite of my hunger, I should have liked to throw my bread against a wall. Some instants after, two squadrons of Polish lancers passed, going up the river; then, behind them, five or six generals, and among the number Prince Poniatowski. He was a man of fifty years old, rather tall, slight, and sorrowful looking. He passed without looking round. General Fournier rode out from amidst his staff, calling out, "Left wheel!"

I never felt my heart so near bursting: I would have given my life for two farthings; but it behoved us to fall in and turn our backs to the bridge. At the end of the promenade we reached a place called Hinterthor; it is an old gate on the Caunewitz road; right and left extend ancient ramparts, and behind rise the houses. We were posted in the covered ways, near this gate, which had been strongly barricaded by the sappers. Captain Vidal commanded the battalion, now reduced to 325 men. Some old mouldering palisades served us for intrenchments. On all the roads in front the enemy was advancing: this time it was the white jackets, with shakos on the back of the head and a species of high plate in front where the two-headed eagles appeared that we see on the *kreutzers*. Old Pinto, who recognized them at once, said,— "Those are the *Kaiserlichs!* We have beaten them more than fifty times since 1793; but for all that, if Marie Louise's father had ever so little heart, they would be with us."

For some moments we had heard the cannonade. On the other side of the city Blucher attacked the faubourg of Halle. Soon after the fire spread on the right; Bernadotte attacked the faubourg of Kohlgartenthor, and almost at the same time the first shells of the Austrians fell into our covered ways: they followed each other in file, several passing above the Hinterthor, and burst in the houses and streets of the faubourg.

At nine o'clock the Austrians formed in attacking columns on the Caunewitz road. On all sides they pressed upon us; nevertheless the battalion stood firm till about ten o'clock. Then we had to fall back behind the old ramparts, where the *Kaiserlichs* pursued us through the breaches, under the cross fire of the twenty-ninth and fourteenth regiments of the line. These poor fellows had not the fury of the Prussians; they showed, however, true courage, for at half-past ten they crowned the ramparts, and we, from all the surrounding windows, fired at them without being able to force them down. Six months before, these things would have horrified me; but I had seen so many such! I had become as insensible as an old soldier: the death of one man or of a hundred no longer seemed anything to me.

Up till this moment all had gone well: but how to get out of the houses? The enemy covered all the avenues, and without climbing upon the roofs, there was no longer any retreat possible. This, again, was one of those dreadful moments which have remained in my memory. All of a sudden the idea struck me that we were caught there like foxes being smoked in their hole. I approached a window at the back and saw that it looked upon a court, and that this court had no door but one at the front. I pictured to myself that the Austrians, after all the mischief that we had just done them, would put us all to the bayonet; and it was likely enough. Thinking of this I re-entered the room, where there were some ten of us, and I espied Sergeant Pinto seated against a wall, deadly pale, with his arms hanging down. He had just received a ball in the stomach, and was saying in the midst of the firing,—"Defend yourselves, conscripts: defend yourselves! Show these *Kaiserlichs* that we are still worth more than they! Ah, the *brigands!*"

Below, against the gate, volleys of cannon-shots resounded. We kept on firing, though without hope, when a loud noise of the trampling of horses was heard outside. The firing ceased, and we saw across the smoke, four squadrons of lancers pass, like a troop of lions, through the midst of the Austrians. All gave way: the *Kaiserlichs* took to running, but the long gleaming lances, with their red pennons, flew quicker than they, and pierced their backs like arrows. These lancers were Poles, the most terrible soldiers I have ever seen: and, to tell truth, our friends and brothers. *They* did not turn tail at the moment of danger: they gave us the very last drop of their blood . . . And we, what have we done for their unhappy country? . . . When I think of our ingratitude, my heart aches!

In short, once more the Poles delivered us. Seeing

them so proud and brave, we sallied forth from all sides, rushing on the Austrians with the bayonet and hurling them into the trenches: the victory was ours. But it was time to beat a retreat, for the enemy was already filling Leipzig: the gates of Halle and Grimma were forced, and that of Petersthor given up by our friends the Badeners, and our other friends the Saxons. Soldiers, students, and tradespeople, all fired upon us from the windows.

We had only time to re-form and take again the road of the great avenue skirting the Pleisse. The lancers were waiting for us there; we defiled behind them, and as the Austrians pressed close upon us, they made another charge to drive them back. What brave fellows and what magnificent horsemen were these Poles! Ah! whoever has seen them charge, especially at such a critical moment, is filled with admiration for them!

The division, reduced from 8,000 to 1,500, thus retired before more than 50,000 enemies; not without often turning and replying to the fire of the *Kaiserlichs.* We approached the bridge, with what joy I need not say. But it was not easy to reach it, for across the whole width of the avenue so many men on horseback and foot were hurrying in order to pass, coming from all the surrounding streets, that the crowd formed as it were but one block, where all heads touched each other: the mass advanced slowly, with sighs and hoarse cries which one heard a quarter of a league off, in spite of the firing. Woe to those who found themselves on the edge of the bridge; they fell over, and no one took any heed! In the middle, the men, and even the horses were carried along: there was no need to stir; they advanced involuntarily . . . But how to get over? The enemy made progress every moment. Some cannon had, indeed, been placed on each side, to sweep the promenades, and in front of the principal street; and there were troops drawn up in line to repel the first attacks; but the Prussians, Austrians, and Russians had guns as well as we, to sweep the bridge, and those who remained the last, after protecting their comrades' retreat, had to receive all the shells, cannon-balls and grapeshot. It did not require much sense to perceive this; which was why everybody thronged to cross at the same time.

At two or three hundred paces from the bridge, the idea occurred to me to run and lose myself in the crowd, and be carried along with the rest; but Captain Vidal, Captain Bretonville, and other veterans, said, "The first who leaves the ranks will be fired upon!" What a fearful thing to be so near, and yet think, "I *must* stay where I am!"

All this took place between eleven o'clock and noon. The firing was drawing nearer on the right and left, cannon-balls began to sing in the air, and in the direction of the faubourg of Halle the Prussians were debouching pell-mell with our soldiers. Near the bridge frightful cries arose; the horsemen, to make room for themselves, sabred the foot soldiers, who replied with bayonet-thrusts: it was a general *sauve qui peut!* At every step some one of the crowd fell from the bridge, and trying to save himself, dragged down others in clusters of five or six together!

The confusion, the yells, the firing, the splash of those who fell into the river, increased every moment, and the scene became so horrible that one would have thought nothing worse could happen; when suddenly a sound as of thunder was heard, and the first arch of the bridge broke down, with all those upon it! Hundreds of unhappy wretches disappeared, and numbers of others were maimed, crushed, dashed in pieces by the falling stones.

A sapper of the engineers had just blown up the bridge!

At this sight, cries of "Treason!" resounded to the end of the promenades. "We are ruined! betrayed!" . . . Nothing else was heard: it was an immense, an awful clamour. Some, seized with the rage of despair, turned upon the enemy like wild beasts at bay, who can no longer see anything and have no instinct save of vengeance; others broke their arms, accusing Heaven and earth of their misfortune. The mounted officers and generals leapt into the river to swim across; many foot soldiers did the same, throwing themselves in without taking off their knapsacks. The idea that I could have escaped before, and that now, at the last moment, I must let myself be massacred, drove me mad . . . I had seen many corpses the night before carried along by the Partha; but it was something still more fearful now! All these poor wretches struggled, with heart-breaking cries, clinging to each other: the river was full of them—nothing but arms and heads were to be seen swarming on the surface.

At this moment, even Captain Vidal, a calm, cool man, whose face and glance had kept us to our duty—even he appeared discouraged; he thrust back his sword into its sheath, laughing with a strange look, and saying,—

"Come—all's over with us!"

I laid my hand upon his arm: he turned and looked at me, but with great gentleness.

"What do you want, my lad?" he asked.

"Captain," I answered (this thought having just then occurred to me), "I have passed four months at Leipzig; I have bathed in the Elster, and I know a place where it is fordable."

"Where's that?"

"Ten minutes above the bridge."

Forthwith he drew his sabre, shouting with a voice of thunder,—

"Follow me, my lads! and do you" (speaking to me) "go before."

The whole battalion, which reckoned now but two hundred men, began to march; a hundred others, seeing us start at a steady pace, joined us, without knowing whither we were going. The Austrians were already on the terrace of the avenue; lower down, gardens divided by hedges extended to the Elster. I recognized this road, which Zimmer and I had often traversed in July, when all seemed one great nosegay of flowers. Musket shots were discharged upon us, but we did not return them. I was the first to enter the river, then Captain

Vidal, then the others, two and two together. The water reached to our shoulders, being swelled by the autumn rains. Nevertheless, we crossed successfully: not one was drowned. We had still almost all our muskets on reaching the other side, and we struck right across the fields. Further on we found the little wooden bridge which leads to Schleissig, and we turned off to Lindenau.

We were all very silent; and from time to time we looked to where, in the distance on the other side of the Elster, the battle still raged in the streets of Leipzig. Long did the furious clamours and the deep echoes of the cannonade come to us; it was not till near two o'clock, when we descried the immense file of troops, guns, and baggage extending out of sight on the Erfürt road, that these sounds were lost for us in the roll of wheels.

CHAPTER XXI.

Hitherto I have related the great deeds of the war—battles glorious for France, in spite of our faults and disasters. When a people has fought singly against all the nations of Europe—always one against two, and sometimes against three—and when it has finally succumbed, not to the courage or genius of the others, but to treachery and superior numbers, it would be wrong to blush at such a defeat; and the conquerors would have still less right to boast of it. It is not numbers that make the greatness of an army or a nation, it is their virtue. I speak in the sincerity of my soul, and I believe that men of heart and sense in all countries will think with me.

But I have now to relate the miseries of the retreat; and this appears to me the most painful part of the whole. It is said that confidence gives strength; and this is true, above all, with the French: so long as they are marching forwards, so long as they reckon on victory, they stick together like the fingers on one hand; they feel that success is only to be gained by discipline. But as soon as ever they are forced to fall back, all confidence is lost, save in one's own self, and the word of command is no longer recognised; then these once proud men, who advanced so gaily to combat the enemy, scatter right and left, sometimes alone, sometimes in troops. Those who once trembled at their approach, now grow bold; they advance at first timidly, then, finding that nothing happens to them, they become insolent, and fall, three or four together, on the stragglers, to carry them off; as one sees the crows, in winter, pounce upon a poor fallen horse, which they would not have dared to look at half a league off if he were still on his legs.

I have seen these things. I have seen wretches of Cossacks—veritable beggars, with old rags hanging about their bodies, an old cap of ragged skin drawn over their ears; wretches who had never shaved, and all covered with vermin, mounted on sorry old jades without a saddle, their feet in a piece of cord by way of a stirrup, an old rusty pistol for firearm, and a pole with a great nail on the end of it for a lance—I have seen such-like rascals, who resembled old Jews, yellow and decrepit, stop ten, fifteen, even twenty soldiers, and drive them off like sheep!

And the peasants—long, lanky fellows, who some months before trembled like hares if one looked askance upon them! Well, I have seen them treat with arrogance old soldiers, cuirassiers, dragoons of Spain, men who could have knocked them over with one blow of the fist. I have seen them insist that they had no more bread to sell, when the smell of baking was perceptible all round; and that they had no wine, nor beer, nor nothing, when one heard the pots jingle right and left like the bells of their own villages. And one dared not even shake them to bring them to their senses—these rascals who laughed to see us retreat; since we were no longer in numbers, but each was for himself only, recognising their chiefs no longer, and destitute of discipline.

And then hunger, misery, fatigue, disease—all attacked us at once. The sky was grey; it never left off raining; the autumn wind froze one. How could poor conscripts with yet beardless chins, so wasted that you could see daylight between their ribs as through a lantern?—How could these poor creatures resist so many miseries? They perished by thousands: one saw them all along the roads. The fearful malady called typhus hung on our traces; some say it is a kind of plague engendered by the corpses which are not buried deep enough; others that it comes from sufferings which pass human powers of endurance. I know not how it may be, but the villages of Alsace and Lorraine, to which we brought the typhus, will never forget it: out of every hundred who took it, ten or twelve at the utmost recovered!

At last—since I must go on with this sad story,—on the evening of the 19th we bivouacked at Lützen, when the regiments reformed as best they could. The next day early, marching on Weissenfels, we had to skirmish with the Westphalians, who followed us to the village of Eglaystadt. On the 22nd we bivouacked on the glacis of Erfürt, where they gave us new shoes and clothing. Five or six dispersed companies joined our battalion; almost all were conscripts who seemed to have nothing left but breath. Our new clothes and shoes hung on us as on clothes-horses; but that did not prevent us from feeling the pleasant warmth of these garments, and we began to revive.

We had to march again on the 22nd, and on the following days we passed Gotha, Teitlaben, Eisenach, Salmünster. The Cossacks watched us from their wretched nags; some hussars gave them chase, and they ran away like thieves; but returned directly after.

Many of our comrades had the bad habit of marauding in the evenings whilst we were bivouacking. They often picked up something; but as there were always some missing at the roll-call next day, the sentinels had orders given them to fire on those who straggled from the line.

As for me, I had had fever ever since we left Leipzig; it went on increasing, and I shivered day and night. I had become so weak, that I could scarcely rise in the morning to start on our march again. Zébédé looked sorrowfully at me, and sometimes said, "Courage, Joseph, courage! we shall return to our own country somehow!"

These words re-animated me; I felt a glow rising to my face. "Yes, yes, we will return to our country," I said: "I must see home again!" and I wept. Zébédé carried my knapsack; when I was quite tired out, he would say,—

"Lean upon my arm. Every day we're getting nearer now, Joseph. Fifteen stages or so, what is that?"

He revived my heart with his words; but I had no longer the strength to carry my musket: it seemed to me heavy as lead. I could no longer eat; my knees trembled: nevertheless, I did not yet despair; I said to myself, "'Tis nothing: when I see the Phalsbourg church-spire, my fever will pass away. I shall breathe good air, and Catherine will nurse me. All will go well: we shall be married."

I saw others like myself who dropped on the road; but I did not consider myself nearly so ill as they. I was still keeping up a good heart, when at three leagues from Fulda, on the Salmünster road, during a halt, we learned that 50,000 Bavarians had just thrown themselves across our line of retreat, and that they were posted in large forests which we must pass through. This news was the finishing stroke: I had now no longer the power to advance, nor to aim, nor to defend myself with the bayonet, and felt that all my trouble in coming so far was thrown away. Still I made one more effort when we were ordered to march, and I attempted to march.

"Come, Joseph," said Zébédé, "come, courage!"

But I could not succeed, and I began to sob, crying, "I can't."

"Do get up!" he said.

"I can't—O God! I can't." I clung to his arm,

and tears flowed down his long nose: he tried to carry me, but he was too feeble. Then I tried to hold him, crying to him, " Zébédé, don't abandon me!"

Captain Vidal approached, and looking sadly at me, "Come, my lad," said he, "the ambulances will pass in half an hour: they will take you up."

I knew but too well what that meant; so I put my arms round Zébédé, to draw him close to me, and I whispered in his ear, "Listen: you will embrace Catherine for me: you promise me? Tell her that I died embracing her, and give her this farewell kiss."

"Yes," he said, sobbing very low. "Yes, I will tell her. Oh, my poor Joseph!"

I could not let him go; he himself placed me on the ground, and went away very quickly without turning his head. The column moved on. I gazed long after it, as one gazes after the last hope in life departing. The stragglers of the battalion were lost in a hollow. Then I closed my eyes. Not till an hour after, or even longer, was I woke up by the sound of cannon; when I saw a division of the guard pass on the road at double-quick time, with waggons and artillery. I saw some invalids on the waggons, and I cried, "Take me—take me!"

But no one heeded my cries: they all passed on; and the noise of the cannonading increased. More than 10,000 men passed thus, cavalry and infantry. I had no more strength to call. At length, the last of all these corps arrived; I watched the knapsacks and the shakos moving on to the descent, then disappearing, and I was preparing for my last sleep, when I again heard a loud noise on the road. It came from five or six pieces, drawn by stout horses at a gallop, the gunners right and left, sabre in hand; then came the waggons. I had no more hope in these than in the others; and yet I kept looking, till beside one of these pieces I saw a tall, thin, red-haired man, a quartermaster, and I recognized Zimmer, my old Leipzig comrade. He passed without seeing me; but then I called out with all my might, "Christian! Christian!"

In spite of the sound of the cannon he stopped, turned, and perceived me at the foot of a tree: he opened his eyes wide. "Christian!" I cried, "have pity on me!"

Then he came up, looked at me, and turned pale. "What! is it you, my poor Joseph?" he said, and sprang from his horse. He took me in his arms like a child, calling out to the men who led the last waggon, "Halt! stop!"

Then, embracing me, he placed me in this waggon, with my head on a knapsack. I saw him, too, spread a thick cavalry-cloak over my feet and legs, saying, "Come, go on. It's hot work down there!"

This is all that I remember; for directly after I lost consciousness. I fancy, indeed, that I heard afterwards as it were the rolling of a storm, shouts, orders, and even that I saw the tops of great fir-trees defiling in the air, in the middle of the night; but all this is for me but a dream. What is certain is, that behind Salmünster, in the wood of Hanau, that same day a great battle was fought with the Bavarians, and that we passed over their bodies.

CHAPTER XXII.

On the 15th January, 1814, two months and a half after the battle of Hanau, I awoke in a comfortable bed in a small well-warmed bedroom. Looking at the beams of the ceiling above me, then at the little windows, where the frost spread out its white wreaths, I said to myself, "It's winter!" At the same time I heard, as it seemed, the sound of volleying cannon, and the crackling of a fire on the hearth. In a few moments, turning myself round, I saw a pale young woman sitting beside the hearth, her hands crossed on her knees, and I recognized Catherine! I recognized, too, the chamber where I had passed such happy Sundays before I started for the war. The noise of the cannon alone, recurring from minute to minute, made me afraid that I was still dreaming.

For a long while I watched Catherine, who seemed to me very beautiful. I thought, "Where, then, is Aunt

Grédel? How did I come back to my own country? Are Catherine and I then married? My God, if only this be not a dream!"

At last, taking courage, I called quite gently, "Catherine!" Then she, turning her head, exclaimed, "Joseph!—do you recognize me?"

"Yes," I said, holding out my hand.

She approached trembling, and I held her in a long embrace. We sobbed together. Suddenly the cannon began to roar, and I felt my heart sink.

"What is it I hear, Catherine?" I asked.

"It's the guns of Phalsbourg," she said, embracing me still more closely.

"The guns?"

"Yes; the town is besieged."

"Phalsbourg?—Then the enemy is in France?"

I could not speak another word.

And thus so many sufferings, so many tears, two millions of men sacrificed on the battle-field—all had resulted only in the invasion of our country!

For more than an hour, in spite of the joy I felt at holding in my arms her whom I loved, this frightful thought never quitted me for a moment; and even now, old and grey as I am, it returns to me with bitterness.

Yes, this is what we have seen, we old men; and it is well that the young should know it. We have seen the German, the Russian, the Swede, the Spaniard, the Englishman, masters of France, garrisoning our cities, taking from our fortresses whatever suited them, insulting our soldiers, changing our flag, and sharing amongst themselves not only our conquests since 1804, but even those of the Republic. It was paying dear for ten years of glory!

But let us not speak of these things; the future will be our judge: it will say that after Lützen and Bautzen our enemies offered to leave us Belgium, a part of Holland, all the left bank of the Rhine as far as Bâle, with Savoy and the kingdom of Italy, and that the Emperor refused to accept these terms (which, nevertheless, were exceedingly favourable), all because he set the satisfaction of his pride before the happiness of France.

To return to my story. Fifteen days after the battle of Hanau, thousands of carts laden with the sick and the wounded, proceeded to defile along the road from Strasbourg to Nancy: they extended in one single file from the extremity of Alsace to Lorraine. Aunt Grédel and Catherine, at their door, watched this funeral train stream by: their thoughts I have no need to tell! More than twelve hundred carts had passed, and I was in none of them. Thousands of fathers and mothers, assembling from twenty leagues all round, watched thus along the road. How many went home again without having found their child!

The third day Catherine recognized me in one of those basket-carts that come from Mayence, in the midst of several other wretches like myself, with hollow cheeks, the skin clinging to their bones, dying of hunger.

"It's he! it's Joseph!" she cried from a distance.

But no one would believe her: Aunt Grédel had to look at me a long time before answering,—

"Yes, 'tis he!—let him be taken out—it's our Joseph!"

She had me conveyed into their house, and watched me day and night. I wanted nothing but water: I was always crying, "Water, water!" Nobody in the village believed that I should recover; but the happiness of breathing the air of my own country and seeing again those I loved, saved me.

About six months after, on the 15th July, 1814, we were married, Catherine and I. M. Goulden, who loved us like his children, had made me his partner ; we lived altogether in the same nest : in short, we were the happiest beings in the world.

The wars were now ended. The Allies had moved back to their own countries, stage by stage ; the Emperor had gone to the isle of Elba, and the king, Louis XVIII., had given us rational liberty. Once more it was the happy time of youth ; the time of love, of labour, and of peace. We had hopes for the future ; we could believe that every one, with good conduct and economy, would attain to a position, gain the esteem of good people, and educate their families well, without fear of being caught again by the conscription, seven, and even eight, years after their deliverance.

M. Goulden, who was not too well pleased to see the old kings and old nobles return, thought nevertheless that these personages had suffered enough in foreign countries to make them comprehend that they were not the only people in the world, and to teach them to respect our rights. He thought also that the Emperor Napoleon would have the good sense to keep quiet ; but he was mistaken : the Bourbons had come back with all their old ideas, and the Emperor only waited the moment to take his revenge.

These things would necessarily bring many more evils upon us yet; and I would with pleasure relate them to you, if this story did not appear to me long enough for once. So we will rest here for the present.

If sensible persons tell me I have done well to write the history of my campaign of 1813, and that it may give youth some new lights as to the vanity of military glory, and teach them that nothing can make us so happy as peace, freedom, and honest labour; then I will give you the conclusion of these events, and tell you the story of Waterloo.

THE END.

CPSIA information can be obtained
at www.ICGtesting.com
Printed in the USA
LVHW022009120422
716028LV00006B/268

9 783752 589962